CAMMIE & ALEX'S
adventures in
SKATELAND

written by: OLGA JAFFAE

TATE PUBLISHING *& Enterprises*

Published by Tate Publishing & Enterprises, LLC
127 E. Trade Center Terrace | Mustang, Oklahoma 73064 USA
1.888.361.9473 | www.tatepublishing.com

Tate Publishing is committed to excellence in the publishing industry. The company reflects the philosophy established by the founders, based on Psalm 68:11,
"The Lord gave the word and great was the company of those who published it."

Book design copyright © 2008 by Tate Publishing, LLC. All rights reserved.
Cover design & interior design by Elizabeth A. Mason
Illustration by Brandon Wood

Published in the United States of America

ISBN: 978-1-60462-892-0
1. Juvenile Fiction: Action & Adventure
09.05.29

To my little friends who skate in
Lancaster County, Pennsylvania

TABLE OF CONTENTS

FIGURE EIGHT

"Cammie, I see you haven't been working on your edges," Coach Louise said.

Cammie winced. The coach was right: she hadn't. But who needed edges? They were so boring.

"Cammie, you think edges aren't important, but you can't become a good skater without them. Keep working!" Coach Louise said and moved to another student.

Cammie sighed and looked at the hockey circle where she had been doing her figure eights. She hated figure eights. What was the point of doing them anyway?

Cammie glanced at Coach Louise. She was correcting Margie Hilton's scratch spin. Huh! The girl couldn't even center it. Spins were Cammie's favorite move. She went forward and swung her right leg around into a fast scratch spin. Yes! That was real skating! Cammie felt like a propeller ready to send a heavy airplane up in the air. One, two, three. . . twelve revolutions. Cammie came to a perfect stop and curtsied in front of a startled Margie.

Margie sighed. "You're so good!"

Coach Louise frowned and pointed to the hockey circle. It wasn't difficult for Cammie to understand the message. She thought the coach would notice her beautiful spin, but all she thought of was edges.

Reluctantly, Cammie glided forward. Her right outside edge was fine. . . well, almost fine. She completed half a circle and had to put her free foot down. Her left forward outside edge was worse, but maybe it was okay. Cammie peeked at the coach. Coach Louise shook her head and pointed to the circle again, which meant *keep working*.

While struggling with her figure eights, Cammie managed to sneak in a couple of sit spins and a loop-toe-loop combination. Whether Coach Louise noticed or not she didn't say. Closer to the end of practice, Cammie stopped doing her edges altogether and worked on spins and jumps.

"And now, girls, I want to remind you of the competition in Skateland," Coach Louise said. "We will be leaving tomorrow morning at ten o'clock. Please be here at eight thirty so you can warm up and run through your programs. We will all go together on a bus, and your parents can come to Skateland later. Wear your dresses."

Cammie smiled happily. The annual figure skating competition in Skateland was the biggest event in the area. This year Cammie would be competing for the first time. She would be skating to music from *The Nutcracker*. Mom had already made her a beautiful pink dress with ruffles and sequins. Oh, how gorgeous she would look on the ice!

"So I'll see you all here tomorrow at eight thirty. I mean. . . everybody except. . . Cammie."

What? What did Coach Louise say? Cammie thought. Perhaps Cammie didn't hear her right.

"That's right, Cammie. You're not going."

"But why?" Cammie's throat went dry and she had to cough.

"Because you're not ready." Coach Louise's voice was stern.

Cammie's eyes filled up with tears. "But I've been working so hard. My program is ready!"

Coach Louise shook her head. "Not hard

enough. Your edges are very bad, and it affects your crossovers."

"But. . ." Cammie didn't know what to say. Coach Louise couldn't be serious. How could she keep Cammie away from the competition? It wasn't fair! Cammie was a good skater. She could do a good waltz jump, a good salchow, a toe loop and a loop, and her spins were the best in her group. And her program was so beautiful! Her mother said she would be the perfect Clara from *The Nutcracker*.

"See you tomorrow," Coach Louise said and dismissed the group. The girls stepped off the ice. They put on their skate guards, sipped water from their bottles, and chatted—chatted about tomorrow's competition, of course, the competition in Skateland. They would be skating on a beautiful arena in a spotlight, and everybody would look at them. And Cammie would have to stay home. Tears pricked her eyes again, and she shook her head violently. No! She couldn't miss the competition. She had to talk to Coach Louise and promise her that she would work hard on those stupid edges every day for the rest of her life—anything to get to Skateland.

Cammie got off the ice and ran to Coach Louise's

office. Oh no! The door was locked. Cammie turned the handle, but the door wouldn't open.

"Coach Louise had to leave early. She said she had an appointment."

Cammie turned around. Margie Hilton stood in front of her.

"I'm so sorry. You're such a good skater. Maybe next time you'll go too."

Cammie's cheeks turned hot. What did Margie know? She couldn't even center her scratch spin, and her legs were short and fat.

"And who said I wasn't going?" she said haughtily.

Margie's blue eyes became round. "Coach Louise, of course."

Cammie bit her lip angrily. "She was only kidding, all right?"

"Oh!" Margie's round face brightened. "So you're going then?"

"Of course I'm going!" After Cammie said it, she felt better. Now she knew what was going on. Surely Coach Louise couldn't mean what she had said. She couldn't keep Cammie away from the competition. She was only trying to teach her a lesson—that was it. When Cammie showed up at the rink wearing her pink dress, Coach Louise would change her mind and let her go to the competition with everybody else. And tomorrow Cammie would do her edges for Coach Louise to see that they were no big deal. Of course, she would run through her program first.

"So what time is the competition?" Mom asked Cammie as she got into the car.

"We'll be leaving at ten, but I need to be at the rink at eight thirty. You won't have to wait for me. You and Dad can come to Skateland, and we'll meet there."

"Oh, is this how you do things now, going to competitions on your own?"

Cammie looked at her mother and saw that she was smiling. "But of course, Mom. I'm a big girl now. I'm ten, aren't I?"

"You are big! And I can't wait to see you get a medal, maybe even win the competition."

Cammie smiled happily. It was so cool! Tomorrow she would be dancing to the beautiful music of Tchaikovsky in her gorgeous dress, and everybody would be looking at her. Cammie couldn't wait for tomorrow to begin.

"Don't forget your skate guards!" Mom shouted from the lobby. She was putting on her coat ready to walk out the door.

"I got them!" Cammie zipped up her skating bag. Everything was there: her skates with soakers on, skate guards, a bottle of water, a Twix bar, a box of tissues. Cammie hung the bag on her shoulder and ran to the car after her mother.

It was a beautiful winter day. The sun hung over the tops of the snow-covered hills, yellow and bright like a gold medal. It was cold, so Cammie zipped up her red parka and put on her gloves.

"Be sure you're warmed up, and try to run through the whole program at least twice," Mom said.

"Okay." Cammie looked at the trees whoosh by and smiled happily. The red brick building of the rink emerged from around the corner.

"Here's a little money for you in case you want to buy candy or something at Skateland." Mom slipped a ten-dollar bill into Cammie's hand.

"Thanks, Mom." Cammie grabbed her bag and jumped out of the car.

"I'll see you at Skateland. Skate well!"

Cammie waved at her mother and ran through the door into the locker room. Seven girls were already there, putting on their dresses. When Cammie appeared, the girls stopped chatting.

"So Coach Louise allowed you to come after all?" one of them said.

Cammie smirked. "Why should you even ask?" *Stupid girls*, she thought. Coach Louise had only been trying to teach Cammie a lesson, and they had taken her seriously. She quickly put on her Clara costume and ran to the bathroom to look in the mirror. A pretty girl with a pink barrette in her long dark hair smiled back at her. Cammie stuck her tongue out at the girl, did a quick pirouette on the floor, and ran back to the locker room to put on her skates. Last night Cammie's mother had put some white shoe polish on her boots, so now they looked clean and new. Cammie took the soakers off, replaced them with skate guards, and walked out of the locker room.

The girls were already on the ice. Cammie went around the rink twice, then glided to the middle on one foot and went into backward crossovers followed by a waltz jump. The ice was good, and she felt great.

Coach Louise appeared on the ice. "Hi, everybody! Ready to go?"

The girls shouted, "Yes!" in perfect unison.

"I'm going to have each of you skate your program now," Coach Louise said. "While one of you is doing the routine, I want the rest of you to stay away from the middle."

One by one, the girls came to the center of the rink to skate their programs. Cammie didn't even look at them. She was busy practicing her own moves in the corner. Everything went well. She didn't miss a single jump, and her spins were perfectly centered.

"All right, girls. I think we're ready to go!" Coach Louise shouted. "You can change and get on the bus. We're leaving in ten minutes."

The girls screamed and rushed to the exit. Cammie stayed in the corner. Coach Louise hadn't asked her to skate her program. She must have forgotten.

"Coach Louise!" Cammie skated up to her. "You forgot about me!"

The coach looked Cammie straight in the eyes. "No, I didn't. You're not going. I thought I made it perfectly clear yesterday."

"But, but. . ." Cammie forgot everything she was going to tell Coach Louise. "I. . . I'll practice my edges. I promise!"

The coach eyed her coldly. "That's good. You'll go to the next competition."

"No, but. . . How about this one?" She remembered what she was supposed to say. "Coach Louise, please, please, let me go. If you do, I'll practice edges every day for the rest of my life."

The coach's eyes twinkled. "Really? How come I didn't see you working on your figure eight today?"

Oh no! How could it happen? Cammie thought. Yesterday Cammie had decided that she would really focus on edges during the last practice before the competition so Coach Louise could see that she was serious about them, but when Cammie stepped on the ice, she completely forgot. She got carried away by the ice, by the music, by her beautiful dress.

"I have my new dress on," Cammie muttered. It couldn't be true. Coach Louise couldn't leave her behind.

"Keep it till the next competition." Coach Louise looked at the exit where the girls were waiting. "If you want to stay here and practice, that's fine. I'll see you later."

And with those words, Coach Louise walked off the ice, leaving Cammie with her mouth wide open. No, the coach wasn't kidding. She was really going away to Skateland, and all the girls were going with her—everybody except Cammie!

ALEX

ammie stood in the middle of the rink with tears running down her cheeks. After Coach Louise and the girls left, she let herself go. How terrible! She wouldn't be competing in Skateland. She wouldn't be skating on the beautiful glittery ice to Tchaikovsky's music. Her parents wouldn't see her compete. And. . . oh no! Mom and Dad would go to Skateland to watch her skate and she wouldn't be there. What would she tell them? That she had been turned down? Her parents thought she was the best skater at the rink. At the thought of her parents going to Skateland and not finding her there, Cammie began to sob.

"Hey, what's wrong?"

Cammie dabbed her eyes with a glove. The last

thing she wanted was for someone to see her bawling like a baby.

"It can't be that bad, you know."

Cammie looked up. A boy in a navy blue skating outfit stood in front of her and studied her tear-stricken face. Cammie knew the boy. He was a couple of years older than her and skated in a more advanced group; from what she remembered, he was a very good skater. Cammie even remembered that the boy's name was Alex.

"You're Alex," she said.

Alex nodded. "That's right. And you're Cammie. I remember you. Good scratch spin."

Cammie's cheeks felt pleasantly warm. "Thank you! But. . ." Oh no! What was the use of having a good scratch spin if no one could see it? Cammie's eyes filled up with tears again.

"So Coach Louise hasn't taken you to the competition, and now you're crying?" Alex said slowly.

Cammie got mad. He was teasing her. "Wouldn't you be crying?" she snapped.

Alex smirked. "Am I?"

"But. . ." Cammie wrinkled her nose, "are you saying that you've been turned down too?"

"Yup!" Alex looked to the side, but Cammie could see his lower lip twist. He didn't look happy.

"I'm sorry," Cammie said. "I saw you skate. You're good."

Alex shrugged. "That's what I thought. I have all of my single jumps up to the axel, and I've landed a double salchow and a double toe loop a couple of times."

"So what's your problem?"

Alex drew a perfect circle on the ice with his toe pick. "Haven't you figured it out by now? The edges."

Cammie gasped. "The edges? You too?"

Alex nodded. "Coach Louise told me to stay here and practice my edges."

Cammie shook her head. "I'm so sorry."

Alex kicked the ice with his toe pick. "I don't care. I'm going anyway."

Cammie looked up. "Going where?"

"To Skateland. To the competition."

Cammie looked at his skating outfit and perfectly polished black boots. "But you can't go to Skateland alone."

"And why not?"

"I don't know. It's far. You don't have a car, and the bus is gone."

Alex winked at her. "I know a way. Want to come?"

"Me? To Skateland?" Cammie's heart began to race. Was Alex serious? Could they really get to the competition somehow? "But Alex, even if we get there, Coach Louise won't let us compete."

Alex shook his head vigorously. "That isn't true. Everybody who registers to compete can go out and skate. You're not required to have a coach with you. We'll just get there and skate our programs, and everybody will see that we're not any worse than the other kids. Come on. They left us behind, and we're good skaters. Do you think it's fair? Do you?"

Cammie was trying to think. Of course it wasn't fair. If Margie Hilton deserved to compete, how much more did she, Cammie Wester? And if it was really okay to skate without a coach's permission, she was all for it, but what would her parents say?

"Now what're you thinking about?" Alex asked impatiently.

"I don't know. What will Mom and Dad say when they see me skate without Coach Louise's permission?"

"How will they know? Once you're on the ice, no one will care."

That was true. Cammie nodded. Yes, she would go with Alex and skate. Her tears dried and she smiled at the boy.

"That's good. Come on!" Alex led her off the rink.

"But how'll we get to Skateland?" Cammie tried to slow down.

Alex stopped and looked around. They were the only two skaters on the ice. Everyone else had gone to the competition. The rink looked strangely large, and the ice was scratched after so many skaters had practiced their programs on it.

"I know a secret," Alex whispered. "There is a secret passage to Skateland."

Cammie's mouth went dry. "A secret passage?"

"Oh yes." Alex turned around as though afraid that someone would overhear him. The rink was still empty. Half of the lights on the ceiling were already off, and it gave the rink a slightly mysterious glow.

"You see, yesterday when Coach Louise told me I wasn't going to the competition, I knew right away that she meant it. I was sure I could do nothing to change her mind," Alex said.

Cammie sighed. Only now did she realize how stupid she had been in hoping that Coach Louise would allow her to compete. Their coach was very strict.

"Anyway," Alex went on, "I knew I had to get

to Skateland somehow. I knew Mom wouldn't want to drive me there, because I'd already told her that everybody would be going by bus. I had no idea what to do. And then I heard Coach Louise talk to our Zamboni driver. You know him, don't you?"

Cammie nodded. "Sure."

"Yes, he told her something that I found interesting." Alex looked around again, bent down, and whispered in Cammie's ear, "All rinks in the world are connected. You can get to any rink if you don't step off the ice."

Cammie winced. "I don't understand."

"I don't either," Alex said, "but that's what the man said. It was something like. . . hang on, 'Skating is like a country of its own. Those who skate are all linked together by a secret bond. Every rink in the skating world is yours.' That's what he said."

Cammie shrugged. "And what does it mean?"

"Well, he told Coach Louise that she and her skaters didn't need a bus. They could get to Skateland by following the Zamboni. It would be easier and faster. Picture this, it takes two hours on a bus and only about fifteen minutes if you skate behind the Zamboni."

Cammie felt her mouth open wide. "Cool!"

"Yes, but Coach Louise didn't agree with him.

She said, 'Oh no, it's not safe. What if someone slips off the ice? Then what?'"

"What?" Cammie muttered.

Alex bit his lip. "That I don't know. And the man wouldn't tell. He only said, 'Make sure no one slips off.' And Coach Louise said, 'I can't take this kind of risk with the children. They're my responsibility.'"

Cammie stared at Alex. "So?"

He pulled her by the hand. "So we'll get to Skateland straight from our rink. We'll follow the Zamboni."

"But what if we slip off the ice?"

Alex brushed her off. "'Course we won't. Now go get your stuff!"

Cammie ran to the locker room, hastily put her things into her skate bag, and returned to the ice. Alex was already waiting with his backpack on. "Come on!"

"But where're we going?"

Alex didn't lead Cammie toward the exit. Instead, the two of them skated to the left side of the rink, toward the gate from which the Zamboni usually came out to clean the ice.

Alex cast another furtive look around at the empty rink. "Good!" he whispered and pushed a big black button on the gate. The gate slid up, and Cammie saw the black and yellow Zamboni, its headlights off. It looked as though it were taking a nap before the hard work of cleaning the rink. The driver was nowhere in sight.

Cammie rose on her toe picks and tried to look inside, but the machine was too high. All she could see was its battered black and yellow side.

"We'll have to follow the machine," Alex said. "Do you think you can skate on the tracks behind it?"

Cammie looked at the floor. Two tracks wide enough for Zamboni tires started at the entrance to the rink and disappeared behind a thick curtain on the other side. Only the tracks were covered with ice; the rest of the floor was concrete. Cammie stepped on the tracks. The ice was perfectly smooth. "Easy enough!" she said excitedly.

Alex bent down and examined the tires. He shook his head. "It's more difficult than I thought. Remember, we must be careful not to slide off the tracks. If we leave the ice, the connection will be broken. Besides, the Zamboni moves faster than we skate. It may shake us off easily."

"I can go really fast," Cammie said.

"Not fast enough. Besides, the tracks are too narrow. And if we don't follow the machine, we won't find the way to Skateland. Even if we slip off the tracks for a moment, we'll get lost. Tell you what, let's try to get inside. There is enough room behind the driver's seat, and we can hide there."

Alex grabbed the rim of the machine, pulled himself up, and rolled over and inside the Zamboni. "It's okay. There's plenty of room here. Come on in!"

Cammie tried to follow Alex, but her arms weren't strong enough to hold her weight. On top of that, her skates kept sliding off the tracks, never giving her a firm grip of the ground to push off.

"Here! Grab my hand!" Alex bent down and pulled Cammie inside. The machine floor was hard and slightly rusty, perhaps because of hours on ice.

"How do you know the Zamboni is going to Skateland now?" Cammie asked as she positioned herself as comfortably as she could behind the driver's seat.

Alex shrugged. "And where else? Where is the biggest competition going to take place?"

That made sense. Cammie wanted to ask something else, but at that moment, the door leading to the rink opened. They bent down as low as they could, desperately trying not to breathe. The Zamboni driver appeared; he was tall and big in his ski pants and a heavy jacket.

The Zamboni driver was an old man, so old that no one at the rink remembered his name. He was a big man with a bald head and a long gray mustache. Because of his mustache, the kids called him Mr. Walrus behind his back. Nobody knew when the man smiled and when he was upset. His eyes were almost hidden under thick, bushy eyebrows, and a white beard covered his mouth completely. All the children at the rink were afraid of Mr. Walrus, although he had never done anything wrong. He would come into the rink on his Zamboni at the end of each practice, and everybody knew it was time to leave the ice. If some kid got caught in the routine of practicing a difficult move and was reluctant to get off the rink, it was enough for Mr. Walrus to glare at the enthusiast from under his bushy eyebrows. Everybody got the message right away. No one ever dared disobey Mr. Walrus. Personally, Cammie had never spoken to the man. Wasn't it amazing that he was the one who could show them the way to Skateland?

The man squinted around the room, as though trying to see something in the darkness of the Zamboni room. Cammie watched him with bated breath, trying to sink as low as she could. *Oh, please, don't let him hear us*, she prayed silently. She was sure the man wouldn't be too eager to take her and Alex to Skateland. He would merely throw them out of the Zamboni and call Coach Louise. . . or worse, their parents.

The man rubbed his big hands and slipped thick red gloves over them. He approached the wall across from the gate, where, covered with glass, was a lighted directory with a list of several rinks. The bottom name was *Skateland*. Next to it was a sparkling crystal button; it looked like a piece of clear ice with a rainbow inside. Mr. Walrus pressed the button and jumped into the machine, turning on the engine and pushing the gas pedal.

The machine moved forward with a gentle rumble, but it didn't go to Cammie and Alex's rink. Instead, it crossed the room and moved along a long dark corridor. It was so dark that Cammie grabbed Alex's hand, fearing that if she somehow fell off the machine, she would never find her way back. The machine followed a long dark pathway with nothing but stone walls on both sides. A couple of minutes later, it took a sharp left. The sides of the machine shuddered, sending a fit of queasiness through Cammie's stomach. She winced and closed her eyes tightly.

When she opened them again, the machine was

rolling along another corridor with faint light flowing in through tiny windows in the ceiling.

"Look!" Alex whispered as he pointed to something underneath the wheels.

Cammie looked down. What she saw almost made her sick. The Zamboni wheels were rolling over two narrow tracks, not an inch wider than the width of the tires. All around them, however, was a ravine so deep that Cammie didn't see the bottom.

Oh no! Cammie thought. *What if we had tried to skate behind the machine? One wrong move and. . .* Cammie looked at Alex startled, and he nodded, apparently showing that he had understood.

Mr. Walrus didn't seem to mind the darkness at all. He drove his machine with ease and confidence, singing softly a song that he had probably made up himself.

My Zamboni, you are nice.
You will come and clean the ice.
So that I can come and skate
till it is very, very late.

As scared as she was, Cammie had to fight hard to suppress a giggle. "Imagine Mr. Walrus in figure skates!"

Alex grinned too and put his finger against his mouth. He was right, of course; they didn't want the man to hear them.

The machine approached a tall, wide gate with icicles, snowflakes, and skates of different shapes and sizes painted all over it. The sign over the gate read *Skateland*.

Cammie's heart flipped in her chest. Wow, they were finally there! Up to the last moment, she hadn't believed she would actually get to Skateland. Now it looked like a dream come true.

The gate swung open, and the machine entered a huge parking lot. Yet instead of regular cars, the parking lot was filled with Zambonis of different sizes and colors. A huge sign hung above the entrance: *Zamboni Parking Only. Restricted Area.*

"We'd better get off," Alex whispered. "We don't want other drivers to see us."

Cammie nodded and looked down. The ice was far below. Could she land without breaking anything? No, it was too risky. None of the jumps she had ever attempted were as high as the Zamboni.

"Yeah, it's too high!" Alex said as though reading her thoughts. "All we can do is slide off the machine." He went first, gently lowering himself to the ground, and he jumped when he was no more than a foot away from the ground. "It's okay! There's ice everywhere. Come on, Cammie!"

Cammie sighed and looked around. The machine had slowed down and came to a complete stop behind two other Zambonis that were ready to enter the parking lot. A tall parking attendant in a gray jacket was looking at a Zamboni driver's papers.

"Come on!"

Cammie bit her lip and swung one leg, then the other around the side of the Zamboni. She grabbed the side of the machine with both hands and let herself dangle along the back of the Zamboni. She looked down. The ground seemed so far away.

"Cammie, go!"

It was easy for Alex to say. He was much taller than her. Cammie closed her eyes, braced herself for pain, and jumped. Whoopee, she was all right! She landed on the ice nicely with both feet.

"I did it!" she shouted, but before she could join Alex, a booming voice came from the security booth.

"Hey, what are the two of you doing here?"

Cammie turned around. A burly parking attendant with a broad red face towered above them.

"We were only—"

"No one but Zamboni drivers are allowed here. I have to file a report about the two of you."

"But we got lost!" Alex explained. "We came here to compete and—"

"All registered competitors enter Skateland through the main gate," the parking attendant barked. "I don't think the two of you are registered."

"Oh, please, let us go. We'll get registered right now!" Cammie said.

The parking attendant smirked, showing two rows of perfectly white teeth. He took a cell phone from his pocket and punched three numbers. "Police? This is the Zamboni parking attendant. We have two unidentified skaters here. . . Yes. . . Of course, I can keep them here. . . Yes. . . Of course I know I have no authority outside the parking lot. . . Yes, go ahead!"

Cammie's heart skipped a beat. Oh no! The parking attendant had called the police, and the policemen were probably on their way to get her and Alex. Oh, what would her parents say?

"We've got to run!" Alex shouted.

They skated away as fast as they could. Cammie didn't remember ever skating so fast. Empty Zambonis with lights off whooshed by and blended into a gray blur. The parking lot was almost dark, so they couldn't see where they were going very well.

"Stop!" The parking attendant had not expected the kids to take off so fast, for he didn't start chasing them right away, which gave Cammie and Alex a head start of about thirty seconds. Cammie wondered how long she was going to last. She was moving as fast as an arrow, yet the parking attendant was faster. He had hockey skates on, which gave him a huge advantage. On top of everything else, his legs were longer.

Cammie followed Alex around the corner. They reached the final row of Zambonis. Two- and three-story buildings sparkling with Christmas lights circled a large square about two hundred feet ahead of them.

"Skateland!" Alex shouted. "There it is!"

"We made it!" Cammie yelled. They were about to enter Skateland, but the parking attendant was still behind them. Cammie looked around. The man was catching up.

"Hurry up, Cammie! Once we're off the parking lot, he can't do anything!" Alex shouted.

"Yes!" Cammie almost skated into Alex, who had stopped abruptly. "Hey, what's wrong!"

"There!"

Cammie looked in the direction Alex was pointing and gasped. Right in front of them was a ravine filled with bubbling water. It wasn't very wide, probably about six feet, but it looked very deep, and the water rolled over what looked like sharp rocks.

"Is there a bridge?" Cammie looked around frantically. The ravine went around the entire parking lot area and turned around the corner. Cammie clasped her hands in horror. How were they going to get to the other side?

"There's only one way!" Alex said as he studied the distance from where they stood to the other side of the ravine. "A waltz jump."

"What?"

"We've got to jump to the other side. How's your waltz jump? Is it big enough?"

Cammie jerked her chin up. "But, of course, Coach Louise says it looks almost like a split jump. In fact, the other day—"

"Okay, let's do it."

"Here?" Cammie shook her head. "Wait, let me practice first."

"There's no time to practice. Look!" Alex got on his left forward outside edge, flew about six feet, and landed on the other side of the ravine. "There! Piece of cake. Come on, Cammie!"

Cammie sighed and winced as she looked at the bubbling water. No, she hadn't lied when she said that her waltz jump was good. It *was* clean and secure. The only problem was that a split second before going into it, she always slowed down just a little to steady herself. So while her jump was high, it wasn't long enough. Would she be able to get on the other side of the ravine? Or would she fall into the cold, angry water, get wet, and maybe even get injured?

"Cammie, go ahead! He's right behind you!"

Cammie looked around and jerked back instinctively. The parking attendant was only thirty feet away. His long legs in hockey skates moved fast, and he held his gloved hands right in front, ready to catch Cammie. He would grab her in another moment!

Cammie closed her eyes. Between the cold water and the angry man, she would choose the water. She took a deep breath. Her heart beat violently in her chest. She glided forward in rapid forward crossovers, went into a Mohawk, backward crossovers, and, finally, there it was, the left forward outside edge. This time Cammie didn't slow down. The man was behind her; she could feel his hot breath on her neck. Cammie swung her right leg as strongly as she could. Up, higher and higher, she flew. For a split second, she opened her eyes and saw the wet rocks under her feet. In another moment, her right toe pick touched the ice, and she skated backward, her left leg gracefully stretched behind her.

"Yes!" Alex hugged her.

Cammie looked back at the wide ravine and laughed happily. It was the best waltz jump she had ever done in her life.

The parking attendant stood shaking his fists on the other side of the ravine. "Violation! Trespassing!" he yelled.

"What if he jumps here?" Cammie said.

Alex laughed. "There's no way you can do a waltz jump in hockey skates. He'd get killed!"

Relieved, they waved at the fuming man and skated away in the direction of the lighted houses.

SKATELAND

Alex and Cammie passed several buildings and turned around the corner. It was so bright that they had to close their eyes. The sun stood high in the deep blue sky over a large square surrounded by two- and three-story buildings—pink, white, and blue. Snowcapped mountains towered over the town like huge walls.

The square was filled with people in skates, yet almost none of them looked like figure skaters. Three little boys whooshed by playing tag. Two girls older than Cammie skated past her holding hands. A short, slightly overweight lady with a shopping bag crossed the street. She came to a T-stop in front of a store with the sign *Smiling Skater* over the entrance, bent down, put her skate guards on, and walked inside. A man with a briefcase skated by looking very busy.

Cammie laughed. "I can't believe it. So this is what Skateland is like."

Alex nodded. "Yup. It's called Skateland because everybody wears skates. People don't walk anywhere; they skate. Fun, isn't it?"

Cammie laughed happily. "I wouldn't mind skating all the time. Hey, do you want to look at the stores? Mom gave me ten dollars to buy candy at the rink. I'm getting hungry."

They entered a small store on the first floor of a light blue house. The sign above the front door pictured two shiny blades framing the store name written in black and white letters—*Sweet Blades*.

Cammie giggled. "How can blades be sweet?"

She got her answer when they entered the store. Though the place was small, Cammie and Alex didn't know where to look. The wall behind the counter was lined with shelves from the floor to the ceiling. Jars filled with candies of different kinds stood on the shelves. The wall to the left of the entrance displayed pretzels in the shape of blades.

Cammie swallowed. She remembered that the last thing she had eaten was a bowl of cereal for breakfast.

"Look! Ice cream!"

Cammie whizzed around. Alex stood in front of a long line of jars filled with ice cream of different flavors. Cammie ran her finger against the jar with strawberry ice cream and then chocolate almond chip ice cream and pistachio ice cream. . .

"What're you getting?" Alex took a ten-dollar bill out of his pocket.

"I like these." Cammie pointed to pastries that looked like skating boots.

"White ones or black ones?" the cheerful saleslady asked.

Cammie smiled. "White ones, of course. I'm a girl, aren't I?"

The saleslady grinned, showing dimples on her plump cheeks. "Who cares what skates you use? I'd recommend both pastries. The white ones are covered with white chocolate, but the black ones are my favorite. Dark bittersweet chocolate. Believe me, nothing can be better!"

Cammie eyed both kinds of pastries hesitantly. "They're kind of big."

"Let's get both and split!" Alex said.

That sounded like a good idea. The saleslady handed them the pastries wrapped up in blue snowflake-shaped paper. "What color laces would you like?"

"Laces?" It was only then that Cammie saw laces of different colors displayed next to the boot pastries. She noticed that the boots had actual loops for laces to go in.

"White laces will be fine," Cammie said.

"Come on!" the saleslady said as she took the whole array of laces from the counter and moved them closer to Cammie. "Forget about the laces in your skating boots. Get something brighter."

"I don't know." Cammie looked at the purple laces, studied the orange ones, winced at the thick brown pair, and finally settled for a pink lace for her white pastry.

"I'll take an orange one," Alex said.

The saleslady helped them to put the laces into their boots. Now the pastries looked like real boots, though a little wild in color.

"Now you need blades!" the saleslady exclaimed as she opened a box of what looked like pastel-colored hard candy shaped like blades. "Just attach them to your boot pastries and you're all set."

Cammie took a silvery blade and pushed it gently into her pastry. It fit perfectly.

Alex slipped his golden blade on the black boot. "I've never seen a pastry like this!"

"You can only get them in Skateland!" the saleslady said proudly.

They paid the smiling lady three dollars each and left the store.

"I'm starving!" Cammie said as she took a bite off her silvery blade. It was cold and had a faint flavor of mint. "What does yours taste like?"

Alex sucked on his blade. "Orange."

Cammie finished half of her pastry within seconds. Inside, it was filled with chocolate cream. "Wow! I've never tasted anything better!" Then she took a bite off Alex's black pastry. It had vanilla cream inside. "I love this too!"

They skated around the square looking at the other stores. At *Smiling Skater*, they bought skate guards because neither of them had thought of bringing his or her own to Skateland. Cammie had left hers next to the entrance of the rink. And while they hadn't had to walk off ice yet, they might still need skate guards when they came to the competition. Cammie chose a pair of pink skate guards to match her new dress, and Alex settled for navy blue ones.

They looked at different kinds of boots and blades—steel, silver, and gold.

"I wish I had more money," Alex said. Cammie only sighed. If she had more money, she would know what to do with it too.

At the clothes store, Cammie drooled over dresses. She especially liked the costume of the Snow Queen. It was white with rhinestones on the front. The sleeves and the hem of the skirt were trimmed with white fur. The dress glittered like fresh white snow.

"Maybe we'll win some prize money," Alex said. "Then we can buy what we want." He was looking at gray and black hooded sweatshirts with *Skateland* embroidered on the front.

Cammie looked at him undecidedly. "Do you really think we can win?"

"I don't see why not. Hey, why don't we practice now? Look how big the rink is, and there aren't that many people."

They were back in the square again. Smooth gray ice glittered under their feet.

The ice looked as though it had just been resurfaced.

"Go ahead. Do your program," Alex said. "Then I'll do mine."

Cammie looked around. Would it be all right to practice her program here? The ice was empty, and there was no one to tell her off.

Cammie went to the middle of the rink and took her starting position. *How about music?* she thought with disappointment. Of course, she could practice her routine without music. She had done it dozens of times at the rink. But it wouldn't be the same. Cammie always felt that music made her skate better. Even the most difficult moves came naturally. Cammie began to hum her music the way she remembered it, and, to her surprise, the familiar Tchaikovsky piece erupted from the loudspeakers surrounding the rink. Startled, Cammie glanced around, but no one, except for Alex, was watching her. She smiled and went into her first spin. As her program evolved, Cammie skated with more and more confidence. The ice was excellent, her feet were light, and she felt beautiful and happy.

When she was done, Alex skated up to her clapping his hands. "That was good!"

"Thank you!" Cammie's cheeks burned, and she couldn't contain a happy smile. What a great idea it was to come to Skateland after all!

Alex followed Cammie, skating to music from *The Lord of the Rings*.

"I don't know why we can't win," Alex said as he skated to the side of the rink where Cammie stood. He was slightly short of breath. His program was more demanding than Cammie's. He even had an axel jump and a double salchow. Cammie thought he had done very well, although the double salchow had looked slightly two-footed. They had finished their routine just in time; the rink was now filling up with people.

"It looks like everybody are good skaters here," Cammie said as she watched a group of ladies gliding on inside edges across the rink. "They skate all the time. I only skate about eight hours a week. How about you?"

Alex nodded. "Same here. Mom brings me to the rink three times a week, and every Saturday, I ride with Jack and his mom to public skating sessions. I know it's not much, but it doesn't mean we can't compete and win."

"I wish I could skate more." Cammie bent down and tucked in her laces. "We probably don't have a good chance with those skaters here."

"Well, you never know. We haven't seen them do any elements yet. Maybe they aren't that good."

The familiar scratching of blades against the ice made both of them look around. A big man appeared from around the corner. He was pushing a wheelchair set on blades like a sled, in which an older woman sat looking trim and poised like a ballerina. Although the lady apparently had problems walking, she had skates on. The man pushed the wheelchair all the way to the middle of the rink, and as soon as he stopped, the woman jumped off easily and effortlessly, like a teenager. She made a couple of laps around the rink and then performed a series of perfect eights.

"Wow!" Cammie clapped her hands. "This is exactly what I can't do. Coach Louise would be happy to see this lady."

The woman completed several three turns and did a beautiful scratch spin in the middle of the rink.

"She had about a hundred revolutions!" Alex exclaimed.

"Eighty-five. But she could do a hundred when she was younger. I could never catch up with her."

Cammie looked around and gasped. She was staring right into the smiling eyes of Mr. Walrus. Yes, there he was with his parka, bald head, and mustache. Cammie expected the man to ask her and Alex how they had gotten to Skateland, but Mr. Walrus didn't seem interested in that particular detail.

"You are a skater too?" Cammie said awkwardly. Was Mr. Walrus's song right after all? Did he enjoy skating after everybody left the rink?

"Oh well!" Mr. Walrus ran his red glove against

his beard. "I used to skate in my youth. I liked it a lot. To answer your question, yes, I'm a skater. I believe we all are, no matter how far we go in competitions or how good our skills are."

"But why don't you ever skate at our rink?" Cammie asked cautiously, trying not to offend the man. He probably wasn't a very good skater, so he didn't want to embarrass himself in front of younger kids.

"Who says I don't? I come early, even before the most determined skaters show up for their practices. Or sometimes I stay late. I get on the ice, glide around, listen to the sound of my blades scratching the ice. . . It makes me happy."

The man looked at Cammie with blue eyes, and she had a quick feeling that he could read her thoughts.

"I don't have to be recognized for my skating skills to enjoy what I do," the man said. "Being on the ice makes me happy. Isn't that why we all skate? Why do you skate, Cammie?"

Cammie looked up. "How do you know my name?"

"I know everybody at the rink. So why do you skate?"

Cammie wrinkled her forehead. Why did she

skate? Frankly speaking, Cammie had never asked herself that question. How could she describe the feelings she had when she skated? Well, of course she wanted to be the best. Nothing was better than knowing that her spin or her jump was the best in her group. What else? Of course she wanted do all the elements well. She also liked beautiful skating dresses. That part was very important. And skating made her popular, even at school. Nobody else in her class took figure skating lessons, and it made Cammie feel really special. Other girls looked up to her, and even the teachers treated her with respect. Yes, those were good enough reasons.

Cammie opened her mouth to give her reasons to Mr. Walrus, but decided against it. Would the man understand her? Probably not. Surely he couldn't enjoy skating as much as she did. No one ever saw him do any moves. He didn't compete, and as for skating dresses. . . Cammie looked at Mr. Walrus's heavy pants and jacket, and her cheeks turned warm.

Mr. Walrus was still looking at Cammie, but the smile had faded from his lips. Cammie shrugged and looked away.

"We all have to answer this question," a soft voice said from behind.

Cammie turned around. The old woman was back in her wheelchair, her deformed hands folded on her knees. If Cammie hadn't just seen the woman skate, she would never believe that her bony ankles could even hold her body.

"We don't skate for the glory of being a winner or for prize money," the woman said. She looked at Alex. Cammie saw him blush and turn his face away from the woman.

"Nor do we care about beautiful outfits." The woman cast a glance at Cammie, and Cammie looked down to avoid the old lady's penetrating eyes.

"We skate because we like being liberated. The only time humans can fly is when they are on the ice. God hasn't given us wings. And yet for centuries, people looked up in the sky, dreaming of getting up there, of joining the birds. They longed for freedom. They wanted to conquer the law of gravity. This is the reason people invented figure skating. It gives us the opportunity to soar above the troubles and cares of the world. Skating liberates us from our shortcomings, turns us into birds and makes us happy. Do you kids understand what I am saying?"

Cammie had been listening very carefully, and,

yes, she could follow the woman. She glanced at Alex and saw him shrug surreptitiously.

"I can barely walk now. Arthritis." The woman smiled wryly. "But I can still skate. Isn't it a miracle? Is it?"

Cammie nodded. Of course it was a miracle.

"And don't believe this man when he says he isn't good." The woman put her fragile hand on Mr. Walrus's sleeve. "I knew him as a young skater, and I see him now. He still has terrific edge control."

Mr. Walrus smiled slightly. "Come on, Wilhelmina. I wasn't a champion like you."

A champion? Cammie looked at the old woman with awe.

"Can you still do triples?" Alex asked the woman.

Alex's words seemed to have hit the lady's tender cord. She puffed her cheeks, which made her look like an old turtle, and snorted. "Triples? Who on earth needs them? Jump, jump, jump, that's all you kids want to do. Don't you realize there's more to skating than taking off the ice and making revolutions in the air? There must be a reason why our sport is called figure skating, not figure jumping."

Cammie saw Alex's cheeks turn bright red. "But. . . you need jumps in order to compete."

The woman waved her hand impatiently. "I know it's a requirement. So jump if you have to, but not before you get comfortable with your edges. You can't do a decent jump unless your edges are deep enough."

Cammie saw Alex suppress an ironic smile. She knew what he was thinking. His edges were poor, yet he was one of the best jumpers at their rink. *You didn't need edges to jump*; that was the truth. Surely the old lady knew nothing about jumping.

"You jump and jump till you are blue in the face. You don't warm up properly, you don't practice your edges. . . no wonder you are such an easy prey for witches."

Cammie stared at the woman. "Excuse me?"

Alex let out the laughter he was holding in. "You're kidding, right?"

The woman's small black eyes gave him an angry spark. "Kidding? Why would I want to make a joke of such an important matter? I've never been more serious in my life! Yes, that's also so much like you kids, making fun of everything you hear."

"No, no, we're sorry!" Cammie didn't want to make the woman upset. After all, she had been nice to them. "We probably didn't hear you right. I thought you said something about witches."

"I said exactly what I meant. Skaters get attacked by witches every day."

Alex smirked. "There're no witches!"

"That's what you say. Unfortunately, denying them won't protect you."

Cammie looked at Alex helplessly. The old woman was either making fun of them, or she really believed in fairy tales. At any rate, Cammie didn't like the conversation anymore.

"We've got to go." Alex bent down and pushed a loose piece of lace into his boot. "Come on, Cammie."

"Bye!" Cammie watched Mr. Walrus push the wheelchair away. Before the couple disappeared around the corner, the man looked around and waved at them. They waved back.

"How stupid!" Alex said angrily.

"Yeah, that witch stuff was weird."

"I mean, Coach Louise has been bugging me enough about edges. I don't need some old folks from Skateland to tell me the same."

"Mr. Walrus isn't from Skateland. He works at our rink."

"Who cares?"

"Excuse me, young people."

Cammie turned around at the sound of a deep

male voice. A tall policeman stood in front of her. He was looking at both of them with a friendly smile, and he had skates on like everyone else in Skateland.

"I hate to interrupt your practice, but I have a suggestion," the policeman said. "I assume the two of you are here for the competition."

"Yes," Alex said quickly. Cammie only nodded.

"Well, the event will take place at the Skateland Sport Center. As competitors, you're allowed to practice your programs there. You'll find the ice much better. This ice isn't that good, really." The policeman did a quick swizzle on the ice and winced.

Cammie and Alex exchanged glances. *This isn't true*, Cammie thought. The ice at the square was good. In fact, she didn't remember ever skating on better ice.

"Where's the Sport Center?" Alex asked.

"This way." The policeman raised his hand clad in a gray mitten and pointed in the direction straight behind Cammie. "Good luck at the competition. I'll be looking out for you." He winked and skated away in long, fast strokes.

"That's good," Alex said. "It's about time we got to the practice ice."

They followed the policeman's directions, and in less than five minutes they found themselves facing a huge glass building that looked like a piece of ice shaped in an octagon. A big flashing sign above the front door read: *Welcome to Skateland Annual Competition.*

"Cool!" Alex breathed out.

Cammie smiled happily. The Sport Center was even more beautiful than she had imagined. She couldn't believe they were so close to the competition ice. How smart was Alex to have talked her into coming to Skateland after all!

"Ugh, ugh!"

"What?" Cammie came closer to the front door, where Alex stood rubbing his neck undecidedly.

"Look!"

Right underneath the big multicolored letters, a computer monitor built into the doorframe flashed another instruction to Cammie and Alex: *Registered participants: please enter your names here.*

"We're not registered," Cammie said gloomily.

"We still want to try," Alex said.

"I'm sure the computer knows who's competing."

"Maybe Coach Louise forgot to delete our names. We were supposed to compete until yesterday's practice, remember?"

"Excuse me!"

Cammie jumped away from the monitor to let a stout lady and a girl a little older than her approach the computer. The woman typed in the name *Rachel Miller*. As soon as she finished typing, the screen turned light blue, and silver letters ran across the monitor: *Welcome, Rachel Miller!*

"Wow, Mom!" Rachel squealed and walked into the wide-open door, pushing her carry-on bag on wheels in front of her. The door swallowed both of them and slammed shut.

Cammie and Alex looked at each other.

"You should have walked in with them!" Alex said angrily.

"Why didn't you?"

"You were closer to the door."

"Well, let's wait for someone else who's registered. Maybe we can follow them."

"Let's try to enter our names first," Alex said, pushing Cammie away. He quickly typed *Alex Bernard* and *Cammie Wester*. The screen turned blue.

"It worked!" Alex exclaimed, but before Cammie could get excited, red letters flashed angrily at them: *You are not registered as Skateland competitors, and you have no authorized entry. Please move away from the competition area.*

Disgruntled, Cammie stepped back. "It didn't work! Oh no, what're we going to do? Mom and Dad will come, and I won't be here! You said we could just come and compete."

Alex hung his head. "I didn't know. I told my folks I would be competing too."

Cammie bit her lip and looked up, trying to keep tears from running out of her eyes. "If Mom comes and I'm not here, she'll be so upset. She'll tell me I'm not competing because I'm not good enough. And she'll be even more upset because I lied. She'll ground me for a month."

"Your mom is tough," Alex said sadly.

"I know. Mom wanted to be a skater herself when she was a little girl, but her parents didn't like skating at all. Besides, she was too tall to be a skater. So she played basketball instead, even though she didn't like it."

Alex sighed. "I understand. My dad doesn't want me to skate. He thinks this sport isn't for boys. 'If you want to be on ice, play hockey,' is what he says. Problem is, I don't like hockey."

Cammie wrinkled her nose. "I don't think I

would want to play hockey. But you're a boy, so maybe hockey wouldn't be too bad."

Alex leaned against the wall. "No, there's no challenge in hockey. All you do is chase the puck. In figure skating, you can jump and spin. And there's music too. It feels great."

"I know!" Cammie said sadly.

"I've been thinking, maybe if I compete and skate really well, Dad will see how great figure skating is and will stop teasing me about it. See, Mom doesn't mind my skating, so they always fight over it."

"I'm sure that'll help," Cammie said passionately. "You're so good. Your dad can't miss it."

"You're good too." Alex was silent for a moment and then he smiled a big smile. "Do you know what that means?"

"What?"

"It means that we must find a way to get to the competition. If we can't come in through the front door, let's look for the back entrance."

The Witch of Injuries

Aback door, an open window, just something," Alex muttered as they skated around the building. "Come on. There has to be another entrance. I can't believe all people get to the building through the main entrance."

Cammie sighed and wrapped her sweater tighter around her body. She was cold and tired. They were circling the building for the third time already, but they couldn't see any opening except for the front door with flashing signs.

"They probably want to keep unregistered skaters away, that's it," Cammie said sadly.

"Yeah, I think you're right." Alex skidded to

a hockey stop, took his gloves off, and blew on his red hands. "It's getting cold. We'd better find something."

"But there's no other door." Cammie looked around helplessly. "Maybe we should ask somebody." She stepped off the ice path that surrounded the building and ploughed her way through the snowy lawn into a narrower ice path. The path led to what looked like a small park and disappeared among the trees.

"Hey, where're you going? Wait!" Alex's voice came from behind, but Cammie didn't look back. High fir trees stood on both sides of the path, making everything look dark, but the sky that glittered through the thick branches was bright blue. Cammie skated faster. The trees spread before her, and she saw a small rink surrounded by a chain of sharp rocks. The ice was as blue as the sky and perfectly smooth.

"Wow! Alex, look at this ice!"

A branch crackled behind Cammie, and a split second later, Alex dashed ahead of her. "Cool! Look how blue it is!"

They both hurried to step on the magnificent ice, but stopped short at the sound of the most horrible scream they had ever heard. "Don't! Don't step on the ice! Go away! Go away!"

Startled, Cammie grabbed Alex's hand.

"What's going on? Who're you?" Alex said angrily.

Cammie looked in the direction Alex's head was turned and gave a sigh of relief. There were no signs of a horrible fight, no blood, and no monsters. All she saw was a very sad-looking boy who sat on a sled at the edge of the rink.

"What's wrong with you?" Cammie said angrily. "You scared us."

The boy hung his head. "You don't understand."

"What would happen to your rink if we skated here once?" Cammie said.

"That's right," Alex said, giving the boy a nasty look. "New people come to our rink all the time, and we never tell anybody to leave."

"Oh, I'm sorry!" The boy's big brown eyes filled with tears. "I didn't want to be nasty. I only wanted to warn you. This rink is bewitched. It belongs to evil Winja."

"Who?" Alex and Cammie said in unison.

"The Witch of Injuries. Look!" The boy raised his left hand and right ankle. Both were heavily bandaged.

"What happened to you?" Cammie said, feeling really sorry for the boy. One injury was bad enough, but two?

"My name is Jeff." The boy sighed heavily. "I loved skating so much. Everybody said I was good. But one day I was practicing my double flip, and I didn't know that Winja was at our rink. I think she did something to my skates or maybe to the ice. I fell and broke my left ankle."

"It will heal!" Cammie said quickly. "I sprained my ankle once, but it got better fast. I could jump again in less than a month."

Jeff shook his head. "No, you don't understand. Winja brought me to her rink, and now I'm only supposed to skate here. So when my left ankle got better, I began to skate again. That time, I fell on a simple three turn and broke my right hand. I got better, but after that I fell on a spiral and broke my right ankle. And then—"

"Why did you keep falling on such simple stuff?" Alex asked. "Maybe your ankle still hurts?"

"You don't understand. This rink is jinxed. Any skater who tries to skate here will get injured."

Alex squinted skeptically. "Really? Let me try."

"Are you out of your mind?" Cammie grabbed his hand.

"Look at the ice. It's smooth. The witch probably has it resurfaced every hour. And besides, who would want a rink where no one can skate?"

"This rink never gets Zambonied," Jeff exclaimed. "It may look beautiful, but it's very tricky. The moment you slip off your edge, you'll fall down hard and get injured badly."

"Why should I get injured? Good skaters don't get injured." Without wasting another minute, Alex jumped on the ice. The smooth blue surface concaved under his feet, and he fell backward.

"Ouch!" Alex grabbed his left thigh.

"Are you okay?" Cammie screamed.

"Yeah, it's just a bruise." Alex tried to get up, but the ice threw him down again. Wincing, Alex crawled to the edge of the rink and sat up.

"Does it hurt?" Cammie said nervously.

"It's not bad." Alex stood up and took several tentative steps in the snow. He rubbed his thigh and gave a sigh of relief. "I can still skate, no problem."

"I told you," Jeff said gloomily. "Winja attacks every skater who comes here. And you're lucky you didn't break anything!"

"I'm not afraid of witches!" Alex said haughtily. "I just slipped off the edge. Let me try again."

He took a step toward the rink, but Cammie grabbed him by the hand. "Alex, don't! Please!"

"Don't! You'll fall again, and this time, you'll get injured badly," Jeff said. His big brown eyes filled up with tears. "The only way to break Winja's curse is to do all four edges on both feet eight times without making a mistake. If you pass the test, then it's all right; you can jump and spin here as much as you want. Winja won't attack you. But one little mistake, and you're history."

"Oh!" Alex moved away from the ice. Cammie knew the reason right away. Alex hated edges.

"But maybe your edges are good." Jeff looked at them pleadingly.

"Do you want to give it a try, Cammie?" Alex said.

Cammie scraped the ice with her toe pick. "I don't think so. If my edges were good, I'd be in the Sport Center with everybody else."

Jeff leaned back in his sled looking very disappointed. "I understand. You'd better not try if you're not sure. After I became Winja's prisoner, many skaters came here trying to break the curse, but they all fell and got hurt. Some of them even had to quit skating forever."

"How about you? Why didn't you quit?" Cammie said.

"I can't." Jeff's eyes twinkled with determination. "I love skating. I believe that one day the curse will be broken. I only need to be patient and wait." He made himself comfortable in his sled and closed his eyes.

Cammie looked at Alex helplessly. "We can't just leave, can we?" she whispered.

Alex looked at her, and she knew what he thought. "Maybe we can give it a try," Alex said grouchily. "My inside edges aren't that bad. It's my outside edges that are poor, but—"

"My forward outside edges are probably okay. When I really try, I can complete a semi-circle."

"It's either all four edges or nothing!" Jeff said without opening his eyes.

Alex looked at Cammie and shrugged. "I don't know."

"Hey, I have an idea," Cammie said quickly. "There's another empty rink behind the trees. I saw it as we walked by. Why don't we practice our edges there? Once we get better, we can do them here."

Alex's face brightened. "You're right! Hang on, Jeff. Nothing is lost yet!"

Jeff opened his eyes and gave them a weak smile.

"Thank you so much for even trying! I've been here so long. No one has tried to rescue me for the last two weeks."

"Do you sit here all day?" Cammie asked.

"Well, not every day, but now, during the competitive season, I have to. I don't want people who don't know about the curse to skate at this rink and get injured."

Cammie and Alex said good-bye to Jeff and went to a smaller rink with dark gray ice. The color turned out to be a real advantage because they could see the tracings of their blades very well. It meant there was no way they could cheat or pretend they were on a proper edge when in reality they skated on a flat with both edges scraping the ice.

At the beginning, things didn't look good.

"I keep slipping off!" Alex said angrily.

"Me too!" Cammie made an entrance swizzle into her right backward inside edge and quickly put her free foot down to keep herself from falling.

"Keep your body straight," Alex said, watching Cammie closely. "You're almost there."

"I wish!" Cammie repeated the exercise. Her feet hurt, but she didn't want to stop. She looked at Alex. His face was red and his knees shook, but he looked very determined.

A couple of hours later, they took a break and finished off the sweets from Sweet Blades. They sat down on a soft patch of snow and stretched their tired legs.

"I wonder how much time we have!" Alex said, looking at the sky. "We still have to get to the competition."

"Don't worry. The competition is hours away."

"But how many more hours do we need to get those edges?"

He is right, Cammie thought. Now she wished she had paid more attention to her edges. She looked at the sky again. It was still bright blue, but Cammie knew that darkness would settle down before they expected it.

After the break, they kept practicing. Their forward edges were already perfect, but the backward ones still gave them a hard time. In about an hour, their backward edges were reasonably good, and after another twenty repetitions, Cammie felt that they had probably conquered them.

"Let's go to Winja's rink!" Alex said as he skidded to where Cammie was still working on her left backward inside edge.

"Let me try it one more time."

"No, that's enough. You don't want to overdo it.

Remember what Coach Louise said? Save your best effort for the competition."

Cammie made a face. "It's not a competition."

"It's even more important. We're going to break the curse!"

They skated back to Jeff's rink. At the clicking of their blades, the injured boy bolted up in his sled. "You're back! I thought I'd never see you again."

"We never break our promises!" Alex said. "Now watch me. If I slip and fall, you, Cammie, will go to the Sport Center and tell my parents what happened to me, okay?"

Cammie clasped her hands nervously. "No, no, Alex, you'll do fine. Go ahead."

Alex stepped on the blue surface. Cammie watched him complete the first sequence of four edges. Beautiful! Wow, even Coach Louise would love Alex's moves!

Alex repeated the sequence seven more times and swirled in a beautiful scratch spin. The ice held him well; he didn't slip once.

"Yes! Yes! The curse is broken!" Jeff did what looked like a belly dance in his sled.

Cammie laughed. "That's right. Hey, do I have to do my edges? Alex has broken the curse, right?"

Alex waved at her from the other side of the

rink. "But of course! You've been working so hard. Go ahead."

Cammie laughed and jumped on the sky blue ice. It held her beautifully, and it was perfectly smooth, yet not too hard. Perfect ice for edges!

"Well, well, well!"

Cammie did a two-foot turn and looked back. Standing next to Jeff was a tall, skinny woman with a mean wrinkled face. All of her four limbs were bandaged, and she skated leaning on crutches. The moment Cammie saw the lady, she knew her name right away. It was Winja, the Witch of Injuries herself. Who else would be sporting all those injuries and bandages?

"So you think the curse is broken, huh?" the witch said in a shrill voice. "No way! It's still there unless you do your edges cleanly. I know you can't do them. I know you're going to fall. Go ahead. I'm watching!"

Cammie felt her heart beat faster. She looked at Alex helplessly.

"Don't listen to her! You can do it!" he yelled.

Cammie clenched her teeth and put her feet in a T-position. As she began her right forward outside edge, her leg shook, but she didn't slip off.

"Fall, fall, fall!" chanted Winja, flailing her bandaged arms.

Cammie ignored her. *Think of nothing else, just the edges*, she told herself. She completed her forward edges and moved to backward ones.

Winja squeaked and scratched the ice with her crutches. "Bad, bad, bad! Fall, fall, fall!"

Cammie wasn't afraid anymore. In fact, her backward edges turned out even better than the forward ones.

"You did it!" Jeff yelled.

Cammie stopped and looked at the witch. Winja's wrinkled face twisted in an ugly grimace and tears ran down her cheeks. "No, no, no!" she sobbed. She waved her arms again and disappeared behind the rocks. The ice lost its intense color and became pale blue, almost white.

"The curse is broken!" Jeff shouted.

To celebrate, Alex and Cammie skated their programs on the new ice. Just as it happened before on the main square, music began to play as soon as they started humming.

"You know what? It's actually easier to skate the program after I got those edges," Cammie said as the two of them sat down on the snow patch next to Jeff.

"Yeah, maybe Coach Louise was right after all," Alex said, making a stern face.

They looked at each other and broke into laughter.

Jeff looked at them with envy. "How I wish I could skate again."

"You will!" Cammie said. "Now that the curse is broken, you'll be able to skate as soon as your bones grow back together. You wait, we may still compete against each other."

They waved the smiling Jeff good-bye and skated away.

The Dark Cave

The narrow street stretched far ahead of them and disappeared in the gray twilight. Cold wind picked up an empty plastic bag and carried it past dark two-story buildings.

"So where do we go now?" Cammie squinted as she looked around.

The street looked endless and not a single person walked in either direction.

"I wish I knew," Alex said undecidedly. "I don't remember the way back to the Sport Center. Tell you what, we'll keep going until we see some sign or meet somebody."

They skated forward, tripping over loose ice

cubes and patches of snow. The houses looked dark, every window hidden behind wood shutters.

"Look!" Cammie pointed to a picture of a spinning skater that hung crookedly on the wall of a dilapidated brick house.

"There must be a rink in that house!" Alex skated up to the building and looked at it critically. "No, I don't think so. This building isn't big enough for a rink. But something is written here."

The street was dark. Even the sun had hidden behind the clouds. Cammie and Alex bent down and read the small letters under the picture of a skater: *For Unregistered Competitors*. Next to it was an arrow pointing right.

"Isn't it great that they have thought of unregistered competitors?" Alex said gladly. "They are giving us directions. I told you. We'll be able to compete."

Cammie smiled happily. Of course. All they had to do was find the way to the special registration center for unregistered competitors like themselves, and everything would be all right.

They turned right following the direction of the arrow and walked along another gloomy street for about half a mile. As they passed a lamppost, Cammie saw another sign glued to its metal surface.

For Unregistered Competitors. There was also an arrow underneath, but this time it pointed left.

They turned around the corner obediently and skated some more along the unfriendly street. The ice was bumpy as though it hadn't been Zambonied for days.

"Ouch!" Cammie tripped over a huge bump and winced. "I hate this ice!"

"Here's another sign!" Alex skated to a tree with bare branches where another sign suggested that they take a left.

Cammie sighed and followed Alex reluctantly.

Seven or eight signs later, they stopped and looked at each other helplessly.

"I don't like it!" Cammie said.

Alex looked around. "Is anybody here?" he shouted.

Deep silence. Even the trees with bare branches looked dead. There was no sun, no wind, just dirty gray ice.

"Maybe we need to go back?" Cammie said nervously.

"Do you remember where we came from?"

"Not really."

"Me either. Listen, why don't we. . . ah ah ah!"

"Alex!"

Alex was gone. He had been standing next to Cammie just a split second before, and now all she could see was dull gray surface.

"Alex, Alex, where are you?" Cammie rushed to the right, where she had seen Alex for the last time. Her right foot slipped; she turned around as though doing an awkward backward three turn and fell. Yet instead of the familiar feeling of her thigh hitting the hard ice, Cammie had a weird sensation that the fall wasn't over yet. A moment later, she realized that she was going down a deep dark well faster, faster, and faster. Oh no!

If I fall now, I'll probably break my leg! Cammie thought, trying to squeeze into a tight ball. Perhaps she would only get a couple of bruises. *Oh, please!*

Splat! Cammie fell with a loud thud on something soft and cold. She touched her ankles, then her knees. Nothing hurt. She was alive, and she wasn't injured. Oh, good!

"Cammie!" Alex's voice came from the darkness.

"Alex!" Cammie squinted but couldn't see her friend. She touched the cold substance under her. It was snow, though not fresh and powdery, but wet and granular. "Where are you?"

"Where are *you*?"

"I don't know." Cammie looked around but still couldn't see anything.

"I can't see you!" Alex's voice was coming from the right; it sounded closer and closer, and then Alex's strong hand grabbed Cammie by the elbow.

"Ouch!"

"Oh, good! It's you! Are you okay?"

"Yes, I'm fine, but where are we?"

"Ha ha ha!" Booming laughter came from inside the cave. A beam of light descended from above, revealing a tall, bulky figure dressed in a flowing red gown with wide sleeves like bird wings.

The creature skated up to Cammie and Alex and stared at them with shining brown eyes. Now Cammie saw that it was a woman, though very tall. Her lips, covered with thick layers of bright red lipstick, curved in a nasty smile.

"Excuse us, ma'am, could you please tell us how to get out of here?" Cammie said politely. "See, we've gotten lost, and we fell into this. . . well, so if you could—"

"Ha ha ha!" the woman laughed again. A mane of coarse black hair fell on her massive shoulders.

Cammie looked at Alex helplessly. What was so funny about the situation they were in? Surely anybody could get lost.

"Welcome to my home!" the woman said solemnly. "Here are another couple of charming little skaters who were caught in my trap. So who are you, kiddies? Pair skaters? Dancers?"

"No, we're single skaters," Alex muttered. He looked scared.

Cammie shivered. It was cold in the cave, but that wasn't the worst problem. She didn't like the lady.

"Single skaters, huh! That's even better," the woman said. "I like single skaters. Those are the proud ones. When they skate, they're always in the center of attention. They think the world revolves around them and their *beautiful* skating."

Cammie flinched uncomfortably. She didn't understand what was going on.

"They think they know it all, even better than the coach," the woman said. "They won't listen to anybody. *Beautiful* single skaters! They come to the rink whenever they want, practice for ten minutes, hang out by the boards with their friends, chatting their way to competitions. They eat snacks, sip water, go to the bathroom—anything just to have an excuse for not practicing. Sounds familiar, huh? Huh, kiddies?"

"How do you know all that?" Cammie asked, bewildered.

Alex punched her hard. "Don't talk to her!"

The woman turned to Alex. "And why shouldn't she talk to me, champion? How hard it is to hear the truth?"

"It's not true!" Alex said angrily as he tried to walk around the woman. She grinned and touched him slightly with her bright red fingernail.

Alex squealed and fell backward into the snow. "Ouch! It hurts!"

"It does, huh?" The woman laughed again, revealing her long yellow teeth. "A little bit of pain won't hurt you, my charming male skater. Now listen, are you any good? Tell me the truth!"

"Yes!" Alex spat out, jumping to his feet. He rubbed his left thigh and winced.

"I knew you'd say it!" The woman looked at Alex and shook her bushy head. "A good skater, right! Maybe some idiot would believe this nonsense, but not me. I've seen your kind, male skaters. The elite few. Kings of the rinks. Every skating club wants boys. . . it's no secret. Whenever a cute boy like you shows up, they pamper him, drool over him, and tell him how great he is. Is that right? Hey, I'm talking to you, skater!"

"No!" Alex squeaked. His face turned red. "You're wrong! You don't know anything! Anything! How dare you—"

"And what don't I know?" The woman put her hands on her wide hips.

"You know nothing about me! No one at the rink pampers me! Why, my coach didn't even allow me to go to the competition!"

"Ah, there we are! Here's a rebel coming to the competition without his coach's permission. Well, you're not getting there!" The woman skated closer to Alex. He jerked away.

"I'll get to the competition, and I'll skate well!" Alex shouted. "I'm not afraid of you! Get out of here!" He tried to push the woman away, but she looked as though she were made of steel because Alex's blow had absolutely no effect on her. She didn't even shake.

"Get out of my way!" Alex yelled.

The woman looked at Alex with mocking interest. "I've always been in your way, my young elite skater, only you didn't know it. And I'll always be with you, because you need me."

Alex stared at the woman blankly. Cammie gave a little shrug. She didn't have the slightest idea what the nasty lady was talking about.

"One thing you don't understand, chosen skater, is that those who follow me always fall. You've followed my signs, haven't you? That's how you found yourself in this pit, and you'll never leave it. You'll always stay here, so enjoy yourself! Ha ha ha!"

"I'm not listening to this!" Alex turned around and tried to skate away, but there was nothing but darkness around him. Alex stopped and looked at Cammie helplessly.

"I told you!" the woman said happily.

"Who are you?" Cammie whispered.

"Oh, you know me too, Cammie!" the lady said with a sugary smile.

Cammie wrinkled her forehead. "No, I've never met you, ma'am."

The woman's red lips spread in a huge smile. "Here's another proud skater. Well, you fell too, Cammie, just like your little friend. You wanted to get to the competition, but you ended up in my cave instead."

"Go away!" Alex screamed.

He picked some snow from the ground, rolled it into a ball, and threw it at the woman. The snowball missed the lady by a couple of inches and disappeared in the darkness.

The woman shook her bushy head. "You really

need someone to teach you manners. Okay, till we meet again then, little skaters." She skated away, and darkness swallowed her.

Alex looked at Cammie. "What was that all about? Who was that cow?"

Cammie shrugged. She didn't care. All she wanted was to get out of the dark well and see the light again.

There was no other exit from the cave except for the narrow passage the evil lady had just disappeared in. Cammie and Alex had no choice but to take the same route, hoping that the woman hadn't set another trap for them.

"There isn't any ice here, just snow!" Alex said as he tripped over a pile of wet granular snow and leaned against the wall to straighten himself. "I can't skate here!"

"We'd better walk. It's good that we bought skate guards."

They slipped on their skate guards and waddled along the path, their feet deep in the snow. Cammie's tights became wet right away, and she shivered. "How far do you think we need to go?"

"There! I see the light!" Alex exclaimed.

Far ahead of them, light flowed into the cave through a circular opening about five feet wide.

The path grew steeper. Panting, Cammie and Alex walked up the incline.

"I understand why people in Skateland don't like walking!" Alex grouched. "It's much harder than skating."

The path grew wider, and the snow turned into sharp rocks. Cammie and Alex walked out of the cave and found themselves in front of a small white house with pink shutters and a red tile roof.

"Oh, how cute! A dollhouse!" Cammie clapped her hands excitedly. "Let's get inside. Perhaps somebody in the house will tell us how to get to the Sport Center."

"Wait, something's written here." Alex came closer to the building and pointed to the sign above the door. Bright pink letters stood out against the black polished plaque: *Proud Skaters' House.*

"Proud skaters? What does it mean?" Cammie looked at Alex. "Are they good or bad?"

Alex waved his hand dismissively. "Who cares? They're skaters, and that's it. Let's get directions from them. That's all we need."

Cammie nodded in approval. "They're probably good. Because if you're proud, it means you want to be the best. If you want to be the best, you practice hard, and if—"

Before Cammie could finish, Alex reached for the doorbell shaped like a blade. The soft sound reminded Cammie of blades clicking against the ice.

The light wood door opened, and a very fat boy of about fourteen stared at them. "Who're you?"

Cammie felt a little rebuffed by the boy's unfriendliness. She took a step back and cast a hopeless look at Alex. Her friend, however, looked perfectly composed.

"All we need from you is directions to the competition," Alex said coldly.

The boy's light blue eyes narrowed. "I can't believe you don't know where the stadium is."

"If we knew the way, we wouldn't have to ask you," Alex said.

The boy folded his fat arms on his chest and gave Alex and Cammie an appraising look. His small eyes rolled in the sockets and lingered on Cammie's skates. "Are the two of you skaters?"

"Yes, we are," Alex said.

"So how come you're not on the practice ice by now?"

"We're not registered," Cammie said quickly.

The boy's lips rounded as though he were trying to say *oh*, and then he slapped himself on his fat thighs clad in blue pajamas. "You're frauds!"

That was the nastiest thing Cammie had ever heard. "We're not!" she shouted. "How can you?"

The boy shook his head in mocking amazement. "You're not even real skaters, how about that?"

"We *are* real skaters!" Cammie stomped her foot. "I've been skating for two years, and my spins are the best at the rink!"

"I'm the best jumper at the rink!" Alex yelled. "I've landed my axel, a double salchow, and a double toe-loop."

The fat boy laughed. "Oh really?"

Cammie didn't know what else to say. How could she and Alex prove that they were really good skaters? The fat boy was so evil! He was trying to insult them. They had to stick up for themselves.

"How about going to the rink together? I'll show you what I can do!" Alex stood in front of the boy, his fist clenched.

The boy totally ignored him. He turned his head back, which was a difficult thing to do because his neck was almost completely covered with fat, and called, "Lucy! Annie! Tom!"

The house shook as though a horde of horses were racing down the steps. Slightly shocked, Cammie took another step back. The fat boy stepped aside lazily, and another boy, slightly slimmer, but much taller appeared in the doorframe. "Is there a problem, Kevin?" he asked in a deep voice.

"No, Tom. I just wanted you to see something funny."

Tom moved away to let two girls out onto the patio. One of the girls had dark brown hair; the other was a blonde, and both were overweight. The dark-haired girl was munching on a Bavarian cream doughnut; the blonde had a bag of potato chips in her hand. Cammie realized she was hungry and swallowed hard.

"Okay, Lucy and Annie are here too," Kevin said. "Do you guys want to look at these two pathetic skaters who have just been dropped from the competition?"

The dark-haired girl giggled. The blonde's facial expression didn't change. She took her hand out of the bag and dropped another handful of potato chips into her mouth. The tall boy grinned and gave Cammie and Alex a patronizing look. "So you guys are losers, right?"

"We aren't losers!" Cammie screamed and bit her lip. She was close to tears again, but she didn't want to give those fat kids the satisfaction. How could they insult Alex and her like that? What did they know?

"You aren't?" Tom looked at Cammie and Alex as though they were insects he was trying to study. "If you're so good, why aren't you at the competition then?"

"We are good skaters," Alex said with determination. "We just don't have—"

"The edges!" The dark-haired girl stuffed the last piece of doughnut into her mouth and clapped her hands.

The blonde smirked, and the potato chips crunched in her mouth.

"It doesn't mean we can't compete," Alex said defensively. "Judges don't really care about the edges, do they?"

Tom winked at Kevin and tapped Alex on the shoulder. "Good point, buddy. If you're really good, you're above all that basic stuff, right?"

"Right," Alex said undecidedly.

"None of us has good edges actually," Tom said. "But believe me, the four of us are the best skaters in Skateland."

Cammie stared at him in amazement. "You are?"

"Sure!" Kevin, Lucy, and Annie said in unison. The blonde handed Tom her bag.

"Okay," Tom said, stuffing the chips into his mouth, "do you guys want to come in? You must be dead tired from walking around Skateland, and you need strength for the competition. It's our afternoon snack time, so we can offer you some food."

Cammie and Alex looked at each other. Cammie had never felt hungrier.

"It's settled then," Tom said and moved away, letting Cammie and Alex into the house.

PROUD SKATERS

The pink house was as cozy inside as it was outside. The couches and puffs were soft; the carpets on the floor were so thick that Cammie felt as if she were walking on cotton, and all the tables and desks were laden with boxes of candy and cookies. Cammie thought that the kids who lived in the house loved comfort more than anything else in the world. As far as she was concerned, that was great, except for the candy.

"Do your parents allow you to eat so many sweets?" Cammie said.

Kevin laughed nervously. "Our parents? They don't live here. It's just Tom, Lucy, Annie, and me."

Alex gave the fat kids a critical look. "You guys don't look old enough to live alone."

Tom jerked his chin up, which made him look even taller. "We are competitive skaters, so we don't have to live at home. Don't you know what kind of people live in Skateland?"

Cammie and Alex shook their heads.

"Skateland is for top skaters of the past, present, and future. Do you understand what that means?"

Cammie wrinkled her forehead. "Not really."

"The best skaters in the world who once medaled at the Nationals, the World Competition, and the Olympics come here to live. Everything here reminds them of their skating days."

Cammie remembered the old woman at the square.

"Skaters who still compete also prefer training in Skateland because there are rinks everywhere. They can have ice time whenever they want. And there are also beginners who are serious about skating and who have talent, of course."

Kevin, Lucy, and Annie nodded and smiled happily. Apparently, they all thought of themselves as extremely talented skaters.

The fat kids led Cammie and Alex to a spacious dining room. Colored photos of Kevin, Tom,

Lucy, and Annie in figure skates hung on the walls. Cammie noticed that in the pictures, the kids were much slimmer. She wondered why they had allowed themselves to gain so much weight. Of course, it wasn't a problem with all the sweets lying around, but wasn't it difficult to jump with so many extra pounds?

Lucy heated up double cheeseburgers and fries in the microwave, and Annie poured everybody a glass of Coke. The food smelled great, and Cammie helped herself to everything.

"Another cheeseburger?" Lucy asked Cammie. Cammie looked at the plump bun but shook her head.

"Have some chips then!" Annie said excitedly and pushed her bag of chips closer to Cammie. Cammie took out a handful and stuffed them in her mouth.

"Are you guys competing too?" Alex said as he took a bite off his second cheeseburger. "How about going to the Sport Center together?"

Tom's face darkened. "We're not competing."

Cammie looked up. "Why not?"

There was an uncomfortable silence. Kevin looked at Tom. The girls stared at each other. Tom bit his lip.

"The truth is, we are the best skaters here, and everybody knows it," Tom said. "We don't need another competition to prove it. "

"Oh, so you have won several competitions, and now you're retired!" Alex said.

The blonde's small eyes flashed at him. "We're not retired. We are skaters; we're simply not competing, that's it."

"Because we are so good, if we show up at the arena, no one will have a chance!" the dark-haired girl said.

Kevin nodded. "We're simply giving skaters like you two a chance. With us on the ice, you'd look miserable."

"Ah!" Cammie looked at the fat kids with interest. "Can you guys do triples?"

"Of course!" the four of them exclaimed in unison.

"Triple-triple combinations!" Annie and Lucy yelled.

"A triple axel!" Kevin shouted.

"A quad!" Tom boomed.

Alex gasped. "A quad? Really? Why aren't you going to the World Competition then? To the Olympics?"

Tom smirked. "Because I don't have to prove anybody anything, all right? I'm the best!"

"But don't you want other people to see it?" Cammie said.

Tom took another sip of his soda. Annie took a box of doughnuts out of the cabinet and placed them in front of him.

"Oh, please, show us your quad!" Alex said, looking at Tom with admiration. "Please? I've never known anyone who can do one. Is it difficult? Can you teach me?"

"Alex!" Cammie said. "It takes years!"

"Piece of cake!" Tom said sharply. "Do you want me to show you? Sure."

Alex was munching on a chocolate-covered doughnut. Cammie thought for a moment and took a sprinkle-covered one.

"Are you interested in triple jumps?" dark-haired Lucy asked Cammie.

"Yes, but. . . I don't have doubles yet."

"It's a snap! All it takes is the right teacher. Come on. Let's go to the rink!"

"Yeah, let's go!" Alex said enthusiastically.

"Put on your skates, everybody!" Tom shouted, and the fat kids disappeared in the house.

Alex looked at Cammie with shining eyes. "Wow? Isn't that cool?"

Cammie finished her Coke and stood up. "I don't know, Alex. Do you believe they can really do all that stuff?"

Alex looked at the door. "And why not? Anyway, it's easy to check, right? If they're lying, we'll go away. As simple as that. But imagine being able to land all those jumps, huh? Maybe they know some secret we don't."

"The secret even Coach Louise doesn't know?"

"Even Coach Louise!"

Why not? Cammie thought. What if the kids could really teach Alex and her triple jumps? Would their friends at the rink be amazed! And Coach Louise would realize how wrong she was not allowing Cammie and Alex to compete. Who needed the edges? The jumps were much more important, and the fat kids were living proof of that!

THREE TURNS

The rink where the fat kids skated had a nice round shape, and the ice was grayish green. The first stars had already appeared in the sky, and their reflections in the ice turned the rink into a sparkling arena.

"I like this rink!" Cammie squealed.

Kevin grinned but didn't say a word.

"Wait and you will see something that you'll like even more," Tom said, exchanging excited looks with Annie and Lucy.

The fat kids approached the ice but didn't step on it.

"After you," Tom said gallantly. "You're our guests."

"Thank you!" Cammie breathed out and jumped

on the gorgeous green surface. She concentrated on doing the best she could, because she wanted to show the fat kids what a good skater she was. Cammie was sure that once they saw how much she could already do, they would teach her all the difficult jumps. She took the T-position and pushed herself off the ice. She wanted to start with some forward crossovers, then do a Mohawk into backward crossovers followed by a waltz jump. Yet, for some reason, her body refused to cooperate. Instead of crossing her feet, Cammie glided forward on her left foot and did a quick three turn. She turned around and tried to cross her feet again. She couldn't do it. Something was wrong. Cammie's right foot went ahead of the left, and she did another three turn. She looked around helplessly.

"Alex! Look, I can't—"

Cammie wanted to say something else, but what she saw totally threw her off. Right beside her, Alex was performing a series of alternating three turns and looking furious.

"What is going on? I can't stop! I can't stop!"

"But why?" Before Cammie could say anything else, an invisible force pushed her left foot ahead, and she performed another three turn, this time a forward inside one. "I don't want to do three turns all the time!" Cammie squeaked.

"Ha ha ha! Look at them!" Cammie completed her three turn exit and looked at the end of the rink where the fat kids still stood. They were obviously enjoying themselves. Annie and Lucy were jumping and pointing fingers at Cammie and Alex, and Tom and Kevin held their bellies while roaring with laughter.

"Oh no! I've never seen anything like this in my whole life!" Annie squealed, wiping tears off her eyes with a yellow glove.

"What idiots!" Kevin did a shaky three turn in the snow and grunted like a pig.

"What's so funny?" Alex said angrily.

"Are you guys enjoying yourselves?" Tom said.

"Of course not!" Cammie bent her knees hoping that once she sat down on the ice, she would stop doing three turns, but the maneuver didn't work. Her knees straightened up themselves, and she went into another three turn.

At the edge of the rink, Lucy clapped her hands. "Cool!"

"What's going on? What shall we do to make it stop?" Alex shouted.

"There's nothing you can do!" Tom said delightedly. "You'll be here forever."

"What?" Cammie tried to face the fat kids, but she couldn't do it because she was in the middle of her turn. Her left foot bent at an uncomfortable angle, and Cammie expected to crash on the ice, but it didn't happen. Something pushed her up and forward into another three turn. *I'd rather fall*, Cammie thought desperately.

"Is this your trick? Did you do it to us?" Alex yelled at the fat kids.

The four of them laughed again.

"Well, as you may have guessed, we are involved," Tom said, still smiling and shaking his head. "Both of you need to learn this little lesson."

"But what lesson?" Cammie squealed, trying to fight tears.

"The lesson for proud little skaters!" Lucy said in a high-pitched baby voice. "Learn your edges and three turns before you even start thinking of spins and jumps! Ha ha ha!"

"Ha ha ha!" the rest of the fat kids echoed and walked away from the rink.

"Hey, wait!" Alex shouted. "What do we do to stop these turns?"

"Nothing!" Tom boomed, and the fat kids joined him in another fit of mocking laughter.

"You can't leave us here!" Cammie screamed. She looked at the backs of the kids that had turned into a blur in her tear-filled eyes.

"Of course we can!" the distant sound of the fat kids' derisive voices reached Cammie's ears, and then silence fell. There was nobody to help Cammie and Alex, and all Cammie could hear was the scratching of their blades against the ice as they went into one three turn after another.

"Alex, what shall we do?" Cammie whined and dabbed her cheeks with her gloves. Immediately, her hands felt cold. "We can't stay here forever!"

"I know!" Alex spat as he completed another forward inside three turn. "Let's try to move closer to the end of the rink. Perhaps we can step off the ice."

They tried their best, but it didn't work. Their feet kept going into three turns automatically, against their will, even when they were close to the end of the rink. The moment Cammie tried to jump off the ice onto the pure white snow at the side of the rink, her body turned around and she entered another three turn. On top of everything else,

Cammie felt the hamburgers and the doughnut doing spins in her stomach. She had a wave of nausea.

"We can't stay here forever!" Cammie sobbed and looked around frantically. "Somebody, help us!"

"Well, well, well! My charming little skaters! We meet again, don't we?"

Cammie looked behind her shoulder at the familiar stocky figure of the woman from the dark cave. The lady's almond-shaped eyes twinkled excitedly as she gave Cammie and Alex a malicious grin.

"You sure don't look as haughty and smug anymore," the witch said. "And let me tell you something, you're not that impressive on the ice. So this is it, my proud little skaters. You have lost the battle. You're mine."

"What do you mean? Who are you?" Alex spun on the ice and glared at the woman. His body twisted as though someone pushed him forward, and he executed another three turn.

The witch sniggered. "See? You can't fight me. And you still don't know who I am, do you? I'm the Witch of Pride!"

"Huh?" Cammie looked at the woman blankly.

"You are mine because you are so proud, both of you!"

What's she talking about? Cammie thought frantically as her feet glided in and out of three turns. *Even if we are proud, what's wrong with that? We want to be the best, isn't that normal?*

"Now listen to me, kiddies! Do you want to get out of these three turns? Do you?"

"Oh yes, oh, yes, please!" Cammie and Alex shouted in unison.

The witch gave them a nasty smile. "Not so fast, my champions, not so fast. There's a price to pay. Now here are your options. You can step off the ice now and live with my little friends, Tom, Kevin, Lucy, and Annie. It means that you'll never skate again."

"What?" Alex yelled. "Quit skating? Never!"

"We'd rather die!" Cammie said furiously before she entered a forward outside three turn.

The witch laughed. "Oh, you won't have to die. I'm not that cruel. The problem is, however, that whenever you step on the ice, you'll never be able to do anything but three turns. My spell is upon you already."

Cammie and Alex exchanged scared looks.

"You thought you were the best, didn't you? Well, you're not. You tried to get to the top without practicing your basics. Now you'll have to pay for it. So it's either three turns or no skating at all. The choice is yours."

Tears streamed down Cammie's cheeks. She couldn't believe her ears. She wouldn't be able to skate normally again for the rest of her life. Just stupid three turns, nothing else. But how would she compete? What kind of a program would she have to skate if she could do nothing but three turns?

Alex darted forward, but the invisible spell threw him into another three turn. "Now wait a minute! We disagree!"

The witch narrowed her eyes. "My gorgeous male skater, did I ask you for approval? I'm not debating with you. I'm merely giving you your options. So I repeat, it's either three turns or no skating at all. This is my final word." She chuckled and looked up at the fading light. "I guess my little skating celebrities need more time to make up their minds. Okay, I'll give you. . . let's see. . . two hours will do it. Till we meet again then!"

The Witch of Pride turned around, looking as though she were going to leave.

"Wait!" Alex said. "We can't do three turns for two more hours!"

The witch did a fast two-foot spin and looked down on Alex as though he were a little insect. "You can't? If I remember correctly, this is exactly what your dear coach told you to do? Is that true?"

Before Cammie or Alex could say another word, the witch skated to the end of the rink. Her stocky figure blended with the trees and faded out of sight.

It was then that Cammie let herself go completely. She sobbed as she entered another forward outside three turn. She bawled when her right foot performed a circle on the ice. She didn't even bother to wipe off her tears when her left foot moved close to the right one at a perfect angle to do another three turn.

"Cammie? What're you crying about? And you, Alex? What's going on?"

The invisible hand landed on Cammie's shoulder before the last three turn was perfectly completed. Within a split second, Cammie was lifted off the ice and thrown on the soft pile of snow at the side of the rink. Another moment and Alex landed next to her.

Cammie looked up. A tall man in a black ski jacket towered over her. There was something familiar in his figure and in the sound of his voice, but Cammie's vision was so blurry that he couldn't see the man's face.

"Mr. Walrus!" Cammie heard Alex's excited voice. "What're you doing here?"

"Just taking care of my business! I'm here to clean the ice, aren't I?" the man said.

Cammie wiped her eyes. "Thank you for helping us."

"How did you manage to make us stop?" Alex said.

Mr. Walrus sighed heavily and gave both of them a worried look. "Unfortunately, I can't break the Curse of Pride. All I can do is give you a short break. By the way, you'd better stay away from that ice."

He helped Cammie and Alex move to the end of the rink, where the three of them took a seat on a wood bench. Cammie's legs shook. She realized how tired she was.

"Here, have some of this." Mr. Walrus took a thermos and two paper cups out of his pocket. He unscrewed the lid, and the wonderful smell of hot chocolate wafted out.

"Thank you so much," Cammie said as she sipped the hot drink. Pleasant warmth spread through her body. Immediately, she felt better.

"Now listen to me," Mr. Walrus said. "We're dealing with a powerful curse here. The Witch of

Pride is the most miserable creature in the world. She needs constant attention and admiration to feed on. When she couldn't get people to love and respect her, she imprisoned those poor kids, making them equally miserable."

"The fat kids?" Alex asked.

Mr. Walrus shook his head. "They weren't always fat. There was a time when they were slim and trim, and they skated well, just like the two of you."

Cammie saw Alex blush.

"I'm not that good," he muttered.

Cammie nodded sadly. After two hours of endless three turns, nobody would feel like a particularly good skater, she was perfectly sure of that.

"Well, they thought they were," Mr. Walrus said. "In fact, they were absolutely sure they were the best skaters at their rinks. They won a couple of competitions, and they loved the feeling of medals around their necks. Unfortunately, they decided they were so much better than anybody else that they didn't have to work hard anymore."

"But it's stupid!" Alex said angrily. "I mean, come on! There are always better skaters. You're not telling us they skated at the Nationals?"

Mr. Walrus smiled. "Of course not. And you're

right, there's always someone better than you. There's always room for improvement. Let me tell you kids, when you win your first medal, let it not get into your head. Never think that you're too good to practice. In fact, it means that you need to practice more, because every medal brings you to a higher level. And the minute you start thinking that you're good enough, that you can't get any better, you stop growing. And you see, there's no such thing as staying where you are. You either get better or worse."

Cammie nodded. "I was away from the rink for three weeks when I was sick. I thought I would be able to do my jumps, but I couldn't. I had to learn them again."

"Precisely. Anyway, this is exactly what happened to those kids, Tom, Kevin, Lucy, and Annie. They became complacent. They stopped practicing. And then they started losing their skills. They got worse. Eventually, they became the worst skaters at their rinks. But the problem was, they had already tasted glory. They had an option, of course. Their coaches told them to go back to the basics, edges, three turns, waltz eights. However, they didn't want to practice elementary things. They thought they were above them."

Cammie caught Alex's sheepish look and nodded. Mr. Walrus was right.

"At that point, the Witch of Pride caught them. It's extremely easy for her to curse a proud person. He's already there, in that dark and wet cave of hers, ready to be attacked. She gave the kids an option, do the basics or quit skating. So they quit. But they still can't accept the fact that they aren't the best skaters anymore. So they allowed the Witch of Pride to take them to the house in Skateland, where they live cherishing their illusions that they are still top-notch skaters."

Now Cammie understood. "And that's how they got fat."

"That's right. Now listen to me, Cammie and Alex. I know you don't want the same thing to happen to you. You love skating. It's a big part of your lives. Did you hear what the Witch of Pride offered you?"

"We did," Cammie said bitterly. "But she said that we would have to quit skating altogether, unless we agreed to do nothing else but three turns for the rest of our lives."

Mr. Walrus shook his head. "The witch didn't give you the whole truth. You can get out of here. You can break the Curse of Pride. All you need to do is perform three sets of three turns on each foot perfectly. If you do it, you'll be free."

Cammie and Alex looked at each other.

"Are your three turns good?" Cammie said.

Alex winced. "Coach Louise thinks they're horrible."

Cammie bit her lip. "Yeah, mine too."

They both looked at Mr. Walrus.

"We can't do it!" Cammie's eyes filled up with tears again.

Alex hung his head. "I wish I had practiced my three turns more."

Mr. Walrus chuckled. "Come on, guys. What have you been doing for the last two hours?"

Cammie and Alex looked at each other.

"Doing those evil. . . yes, we've been practicing three turns, right?" Alex looked at Mr. Walrus with shining eyes.

"That's right!" The man tapped Alex on the shoulder. "And I saw both of you. Your three turns weren't bad at all!"

Cammie looked at Alex, then at Mr. Walrus, then back at Alex. Both of them smiled at her.

"So are you saying that if we do our three turns, we'll be free?" she said slowly.

Mr. Walrus's eyes twinkled mischievously.

"Only if you do them perfectly well. This is the condition."

Cammie glanced at the green ice. "Can we?"

"Oh, come on!" Alex jumped on the ice. He entered a right forward outside three turn without a moment's hesitation.

Cammie watched her friend carefully. Perfect! The turn was big and smooth. The other foot. Cammie flinched. That's where she always had trouble. No, everything was fine. Alex did the left forward outside three turn beautifully too. With bated breath, Cammie followed Alex's movements on the ice. "He's so good!" she muttered.

Mr. Walrus grinned beside her. "Sure. So those two hours weren't a complete waste, right, Cammie?"

Before Cammie could answer, Alex raised his both hands in the air. "I did it! I did it!" He spun and went into rapid backward crossovers. This time, nothing forced him to do any more three turns. He was free.

Mr. Walrus gave Cammie a slight push. "Your turn."

Cammie looked at the ice undecidedly. "What if I fail?"

"Well, you'll never know unless you try, right?" Mr. Walrus said.

Cammie closed her eyes, praying for courage. She stood up. Her legs felt like rubber. *I can do it,* she said to herself. *I've done it so many times before. It's easy!*

She stepped on the ice and went into her first three turn. Why was she afraid of them? They were easy! If only Coach Louise could see her now!

Cammie completed her last turn and looked around. Mr. Walrus and Alex were applauding her.

"Perfect!" Alex yelled, giving her a thumbs-up.

"The curse is broken," Mr. Walrus said solemnly.

"Oh no! Why did you do it? Why did you do it?" The three of them turned left and saw the Witch of Pride kicking the ice with her toe-picks. "It's your fault!" she yelled at Mr. Walrus. "Why did you tell them how to break the curse? They wouldn't have thought of it themselves!"

"Any competition has to be honest," Mr. Walrus said. "And even proud skaters need a chance to redeem themselves."

"I wanted more kids in my house!" the witch whined.

Mr. Walrus ignored her and turned to Alex and

Cammie. "Now go. You need to get to the competition on time."

"But how about those fat kids in the witch's house?" Cammie said.

Mr. Walrus thought for a minute. "They will always have a choice, just like the two of you did. And if they want to skate again, they are only three sets of three turns away from their goal. Now go!"

"Which way?" Alex asked.

"Straight ahead. Follow the signs. They will take you to the competition. In due time." Mr. Walrus raised his voice slightly when he pronounced the last sentence and looked both of them straight in the eyes.

"Thanks!" Cammie said and followed Alex along a narrow path to the street. Before they turned around the corner, Cammie looked back. Mr. Walrus wasn't there anymore. The rink looked clean and shiny with bright silver stars shining on its green surface.

THE WITCH OF FEAR

I wonder how much farther we have to go," Cammie said tiredly. "Skating around would be fine, but this street doesn't have any ice."

The section of the street that was only twenty feet away from the proud skaters' house was ice-free. Instead, the sidewalks were covered with gray snow. Cammie looked at the four sets of footsteps and shook her head. The fat kids didn't skate anymore; they walked everywhere. She winced and moved to the middle of the sidewalk where the snow was more packed.

"Cheer up!" Alex said excitedly. "Think of the

competition. We'll be there soon and skate our best."

"Of course we will." Cammie smiled. Her thoughts went back to her competition, to herself spinning beautifully to her *Nutcracker* music. The picture warmed her up, and she didn't feel cold anymore. Her feet were a little tired, but it was no big deal.

They waddled to the end of the street. It was lined with two-story houses with steep roofs that looked dark against the graying sky. A lonely beam of the setting sun fell on a piece of paper pinned to a post. Alex tore the note off and read *Unregistered skaters, this way!* "Hey, they haven't forgotten us!" He checked the direction of the arrow drawn underneath. "We are supposed to turn right."

Behind the right corner, the gray slushy snow changed to ice again.

"Good!" Cammie said.

The road got narrower and slightly more declined. Cammie's skates carried her easily along the icy path. She giggled. "Hey, Alex, I'm ahead of you!" Her speed increased. Cammie spread her arms like an airplane ready to take off. Wouldn't it be cool if she really flew off the ice up into the sky?

"Cammie, you're going too fast!" Alex's voice came from behind.

She ignored it. She was going faster than ever before, but the feeling was amazing. Wind ruffled her hair, and Cammie felt as though she had become one with the wind. She was incredibly light inside. If she could only glide like that all the time!

"Cammie!" she heard Alex's voice again but forgot about it right away.

The road became steeper. Cammie's body jerked dangerously forward, and she bent her knees hard to stay balanced. Her ankles screamed in her stiff boots.

I've got to stop, Cammie thought. She tried to move her feet to the hockey stop position, but as she did that, she almost lost her balance. No, the hockey stop wasn't the best idea. How about a T-stop? Ugh, that would be even worse. A snow plough? Cammie turned her toes slightly in, which almost caused her to fall on her face. She quickly moved her feet back, and they were now parallel, moving along faster and faster.

"Cammie, we need to slow down! Do you hear me? Cammie!" Alex was calling her again.

"I can't stop!" Cammie shouted, but the ice-cold wind rushed into her mouth and stole her last words.

The speed increased. Houses and trees rushed by like images in a kaleidoscope. Finally, Cammie couldn't see anything anymore. The town turned into a blur of shapes and colors.

"Help!" Cammie screamed. "Somebody help me!" The wind carried her words in every possible direction, but the sounds moved too fast for anybody to discern. Cammie realized that nobody would come to her rescue. She had to think of something herself, and the sooner, the better.

Alex was behind Cammie; she could hear him screaming, probably trying to slow down too. *Maybe I need to sit down on the ice?* Cammie thought. She looked at the ice and decided against it. Her speed was so high that if she moved fast, she would definitely fall and get injured. *Who is doing this to us?* Cammie thought. Could it be Winja again, trying to hurt Alex and her? No, of course not. They had defeated her. She couldn't do anything to them anymore.

Something bright appeared ahead of Cammie, white and soft, and it was getting bigger and bigger. *A pile of snow*, Cammie realized. Yes, that was her chance. The road wound slightly to the right. If she managed to move left just a little bit and then jump on the pile of snow, she might be able to get off the evil decline. But what would be the best way of hitting the snow without falling on the ice? Cammie closed her eyes for a second, trying to concentrate.

Yes! A thought flashed through her mind. All she had to do was jump a salchow. If she took off the ice backward with the road winding to the right, she would surely land on the snow after she completed the jump. Cammie steadied herself on the ice, moved her right arm forward, and got on the left forward outside edge. Before the ice could throw her off, Cammie did a quick three turn and swung her free arm and leg around. Boy, she was going fast. Her heart leaped inside her chest, but the momentum was there. She straightened her left knee, sending herself into the air, higher, higher, higher. . .

Yes! Cammie fell on the soft glistening snow that felt like the mattress on her bed at home. She smiled as she looked into the sky that was blue and clear again.

Splash! Something big and navy blue landed on the snow next to Cammie, sending cold powder into her eyes.

"Ugh!" She rubbed her face with the back of her

hand and sat up. Alex smiled at her, his face red and wet.

"Hey, you made it!" Cammie said excitedly. "Did you jump a salchow too?"

Alex smiled mischievously. "No, an axel."

"Wow!" Cammie shook her head in amazement. "I can't do it. I tried, but all I do is fall and fall."

"You'll get it." Alex's eyes sparkled encouragingly. "You should have seen that salchow of yours!"

"Was it good?"

"Didn't you feel it yourself? Come on, girl, you had enough height for a triple!"

"No!" Cammie laughed happily. "You're kidding, right?"

"I'm serious!"

Cammie jumped off the snow. The road wound to the right. Cammie looked left. A small circular rink with pale pink ice lay in front of her.

"It's pretty!" Cammie moved her foot forward, ready to step on the ice, but jumped back quickly. "Maybe it's bewitched too."

"Wait!" Alex put his right foot on the ice and balanced on it for a second. Nothing happened. He pushed off with his left foot and glided forward. "It's okay!"

Cammie joined him, and they took a couple of

laps around the rink. Cammie tried a couple of sal-chows. Wow, they were really higher than ever before. She tried to become tighter in the air, to spin faster. . .

"A double!" Alex screamed. "Cammie, you've just landed a double!"

Cammie squealed and clapped her hands. "I can't believe it! I can't believe it!"

"If you want to learn a jump, all you need to do is get yourself in a dangerous situation," Alex said, winking at her. "Wait till I tell Coach Louise that."

"Don't you dare!"

"Boy, you're brave!" The voice wasn't Alex's; it came from behind.

Cammie turned around. A very skinny red-haired girl of about her age smiled at her sadly. The girl moved very slowly, barely gliding on the ice. She looked like a beginner who was at the rink for the first time in her life. Her knees were bony and so fragile that Cammie wondered if they would break if the girl took another step.

"You're very good skaters, both of you," the girl said, looking at Cammie and Alex with her big blue eyes.

"Thank you," Cammie said. "Are you learning to skate?"

A tear flowed out of the girl's eye and rolled down her cheek.

"Hey, it's okay," Alex said. "There's nothing to be ashamed of. When I was on ice for the first time in my life, boy, you should have seen me. I fell about twenty times."

Cammie grinned. "I fell only once and told Mom I was never going to skate again. Period. She had to promise me an ice cream sandwich and a new Barbie doll just to get me back on the ice."

"Anyway, it's all about the right technique," Alex said. "You're walking on the ice, see? It's wrong. Try gliding instead. Push off the ice with one foot, then glide on both feet. It's easy, look!" He demonstrated basic stroking to the girl, but she made no attempt to repeat the exercise. Instead, she stood in the same spot crying silently.

Alex turned to Cammie looking confused. Cammie frowned. If the girl didn't want to learn how to skate right, why had she come to the rink? That was exactly what Cammie wanted to ask the red-haired girl, but as she looked at the girl's miserable face, she changed her mind.

"Look, we're sorry," Cammie said. "We were only trying to help. But if you'd rather learn on your own, go ahead. We'll leave."

The girl shook her head vigorously. "Oh no, you don't understand. You think I'm a beginner, don't you? I'm not. I'm a skater. I used to do doubles."

Alex's eyes narrowed in suspicion. "You did? So what's wrong with you now? Did you get injured?"

"No!" the girl whined. "I'm afraid of skating, that's it! I can't skate normally because I know that I'll fall and get injured. I can't do anything. I can't even look at the ice. And it's all because of her, because of her!" She buried her face in her hands and wept bitterly.

Alex and Cammie looked at each other.

"Who're you talking about?" Alex asked.

The girl looked around and shuddered. She moved closer to Cammie and Alex and whispered, "It's because of the witch."

Cammie winced. "Who?"

"The Witch of Fear. She's evil. She doesn't want people to skate, so she destroys them by making them afraid of the ice."

Cammie looked at the ice and was unable to believe what the girl had said. How could someone be afraid of the ice? It was weird. The ice was so beautiful; it didn't look scary at all.

"Now you guys better get out of here, or she'll see you and destroy you too," the girl said, wrapping her green sweater tighter around her skinny shoulders.

"We aren't afraid of witches!" Alex exclaimed.

The girl blinked. "Maybe you aren't. I saw both of you jump. You're good. But I was good too. Until one day I came to the rink and couldn't skate. I never landed another jump. The following day, I couldn't even do crossovers, that's how scared I was. Now I have no strength to stroke. It feels as though the Witch of Fear is always inside me, telling me that I can't skate."

Cammie flinched. It sounded horrible. "What can we do to help you?" she said warily.

The girl waved her hand at Cammie. "There's nothing you can do. Just get out of here before she sees you!"

Cammie glanced at Alex, unsure of what to do. Perhaps it would be better for them to turn around and take a different road to the competition.

"We have to go this way." Alex pointed to the tree-lined road across the rink. "See the arrow?"

Cammie squinted and saw the familiar sign inviting unregistered skaters to go straight.

The girl gasped. "You can't go that way. That road leads directly to the witch's house!"

"Oh!" Cammie looked around. "Sure! Come on,

Alex, let's walk around. There has to be another way to the competition."

Alex gave the girl a questioning look. "Do you know a different road?"

The girl shook her head. "There's no other way. You aren't registered, are you? Then you have to walk by this house."

Cammie sighed. "Let's go then. We don't have a choice, do we?"

The girl's eyes widened. "Of course you do! Go back home. You don't need this competition. Who cares about medals if they may put an end to your skating career?"

"We have to go," Alex said. Cammie nodded in agreement.

"Wait! You don't know what you're doing!" The girl's shrill voice followed them as they skated across the rink and stepped on the snow white ice that led to what looked like an ice castle in the distance.

"Wait! Wait a minute!" The girl grabbed Cammie by the arm, forcing her to turn back.

"And how did you manage to catch up with us if you're so scared?" Alex said angrily.

The girl's pale cheeks went slightly pink. "I guess. . . I wasn't thinking of myself anymore. I was thinking of you."

Alex rolled his eyes.

"Look!" the girl said to Cammie, ignoring Alex. "When you come to the gate, you'll be asked to enter the password. Be sure to do everything right. Then the witch will jump out and try to scare you. Try not to be afraid, just keep skating. If you make no mistakes, she will let you pass. If not—"

"Then what?" Alex said mockingly.

The girl shook her head. "You can't even imagine how many skaters' lives are ruined by fear."

Alex pulled Cammie by the hand. "Let's go."

They moved forward, leaving the scared girl behind. The trees stepped to the sides, allowing them to catch a good look at a big white house with columns and sculptures of the most monstrous creatures Cammie had ever seen. *One look at these, and you don't even need a witch*, Cammie thought as she glanced at the sculpture of a skeleton with broken teeth.

"They're only here to scare us, Cammie," Alex said. "Just forget about them."

It was easier said than done. Cammie half closed her eyes and focused on the sign carved in ice on the front door: *Please enter the password*. Underneath another sign said in smaller letters: *Password: OW8-IW8-OW8.*

Alex laughed sarcastically. "What kind of a password is it if everybody knows?"

Cammie nodded in agreement. "Let's enter it and go to the competition."

"Sure. I knew that redhead was the panicky type from the beginning. Witch of Fear, big deal!" Alex snorted. He looked around and frowned.

"What?"

"Where're we supposed to enter the password?"

"I don't know." Cammie searched for a panel, a keyboard—something with letters and numbers. There was nothing. The front door was cold and smooth, and the patio was empty.

"Maybe we're supposed to write it on the snow?" Alex said. "I need a stick or something."

Cammie bent down. "But there's no snow here, just ice!"

"We can write it on the ice then. Oh, I know, we can scratch the password on the ice with our toe picks."

A wave of realization swept over Cammie. It felt as though someone had turned on a lamp in her mind. "Alex," she whispered, "I know."

"What do you know?"

"The password. It's a combination of moves. You know, figure skating moves."

Alex looked at her dubiously. "What do you mean?"

"Look." Cammie came up to the door and ran her finger against the first combination: *OW8*. It means outside waltz eight, see?"

"Hang on!" Alex raised his finger in the air while staring at Cammie repulsively. "Outside waltz eight? Are we supposed to do outside waltz eights? Now?"

"But of course! And here, look, *IW8*! It means—"

"Inside waltz eight," Alex whispered, shaking his head. "I can't believe it!"

"How are your waltz eights?" Cammie said sadly.

Alex grinned. "Do you have to ask?"

"No, I know."

They stepped back and looked at the house with a mixture of fear and disgust.

"I hate waltz eights!" Alex groaned. "Cammie, you do them, all right?"

"What makes you think I like them?"

"Well, you're a girl."

"So what? I like jumping and spinning, not doing stupid turns."

"Tell you what," Alex said, turning away from the house, "let's go and ask that red-haired crybaby if there's a different way to the competition. There has to be, you know."

"She already told us there isn't."

"Oh well!" Alex looked at the locked gate, at the sky that had already turned dark blue. "I guess we don't have a choice."

Cammie looked at the pink ice. "So it's edges again. Only this time we have to practice waltz eights, right?"

Alex nodded, but before Cammie could say another word, his face lit up.

"What?" Cammie said.

"You know what? I don't think we need any more practice. Watch me!" Alex jumped on the ice, took a T-position in the middle, and pushed off with his left foot. He did half a circle on his outside edge, went into a flawless three turn, got back on his right foot, and completed the circle. He repeated the same on his left foot. From where she stood, Cammie could see the tracings Alex had left on the ice. It was a perfect figure eight.

Cammie opened her eyes wide. "Alex, you're so

good! Why didn't you tell me the truth? You said you couldn't do waltz eights well."

Alex skated up to her. His cheeks flushed. "I didn't lie to you. I didn't even know I could do them until I tried."

Cammie stared at him. "I don't understand."

"Go ahead, try!" Alex nudged her in the direction of the ice.

Cammie stepped back. "Come on! I know I can't do them. We don't want the Witch of Fear to attack us, do we?"

"She won't! Trust me, Cammie!"

Cammie frowned. She didn't understand why Alex was so sure she could do waltz eights. Of all the moves in the field, waltz eights were her least favorite. Coach Louise always told her to practice them more, for she had problems with them. But Cammie hated them so much that whenever her coach was around, she would hide behind taller skaters and practice something else. Sometimes, however, Coach Louise would understand her maneuver. She would drag Cammie to the middle and make her do waltz eights over and over again. That never worked. Cammie could never complete a circle. The tracings she left on the ice looked like a flat cantaloupe or a blown-out cucumber. On top of everything else, Cammie always tripped on her first three turn and had to put her free foot down. Surely a sloppy waltz eight would never satisfy the witch!

"I think I'd better practice first," Cammie said sadly.

"Just do it, silly!" Alex grabbed her hand and led her to the ice.

"Oh, all right!" Cammie made a nasty face and skated to the middle of the rink. The ice had a pleasant feel to it. It wasn't too hard or too soft, just enough for the edges to be nice and deep.

Cammie skidded to a stop and put her feet in a T-position. She glared at Alex. How could he make her skate like that without practicing even once? Alex grinned and waved at her.

"Fine," Cammie snapped and moved forward. Wow, she had never realized how easy it was! Her forward outside edge was deep and curvy, and she completed her three turn without even thinking of it. A couple seconds more and she was pushing off with her right foot into the left outside edge. No problem there either.

Amazed, Cammie looked at Alex. He was giving her a thumbs-up. "Easy, huh?"

"But why?" Cammie shrugged and laughed happily. "How did it happen?"

Alex skated up to her. "Don't you understand? We've been practicing our edges and three turns for hours. And what does a waltz eight consist of?"

"Edges and three turns."

"Exactly. Now let's enter the witch's password and get out of here."

They took their turns alternating outside and inside waltz eights. For the first time in her life, Cammie was enjoying it. *I wonder what Coach Louise will say*, she thought happily.

"Done!" Alex shouted and clapped his hands.

"Me too!" Cammie raised her hands in triumph. "We can go to the competition now!"

"Hold it right there!"

Alex and Cammie spun around. The iron gate had slid up, and out stepped a tall gaunt woman who looked as though she were made of ice and snow. Sparkling white hair streamed down her shoulders and waist and almost to the ground. The woman's eyes were half covered by heavy eyelids, which made it difficult to tell what color eyes she had. The witch's fingernails were about a foot long and curled around her hands in spiral twists.

"You'll never skate again!" the Witch of Fear groaned. Her voice reminded Cammie of the wind howling on a dark street at night.

"But. . . but we've entered your password correctly," Cammie said.

The witch's lips spread, revealing two rows of sharp teeth shaped like icicles. For a split second, Cammie wondered how they fit in the witch's mouth.

"So you think you conquered your fears only because you did a couple of decent figure eights?" she howled. "Oh no, my children, it's not that simple. Fear is skaters' best friend, did you know that? Maybe you were too young to understand it before, but now it's time for you to grow up. From now on, I'll always be with you. I'll never go away. I'll taunt you when you step on the ice. When you try to land a jump, your first thought will be of me. My face will pop up in your mind as you enter a spin. And whenever you think of me, your knees will start shaking, and your blades will slip, and down, down, down you will fall. And one day fear will become so intense that you will decide to give up skating altogether, because it's easier to stay away from ice than succumb to the inevitable. Look at the ice!"

Mesmerized by the witch's words, Cammie obeyed.

"It's cold and hard. It has no mercy. It will destroy you. That's what the ice is for, to kill and destroy. You'll never forget it. Even if you're brave enough to step on the ice, you'll never be able to hold your balance. You'll be like beginners learning to skate. Thus says the Witch of Fear!"

"No!" Alex yelled, grabbing Cammie's hand. "Cammie, don't listen to her! She's lying!"

"Am I?" The witch's eyelids slid up, and enormous bloodshot eyes looked down at Cammie. She screamed and covered her face with her hands.

"Cammie, don't be afraid of her! Let's get out of here!" Cammie heard Alex's voice next to her, but the shiver had spread to her whole body. Though her eyes were shut tight, she saw a horde of monstrous creatures floating in her realm of vision. Dragons, skeletons, and witches swooped by. Cammie whined and felt herself fall. That was it. She was going to get injured. She would never skate again.

"Cammie, open your eyes! Now!" Cammie opened her eyes and looked into the familiar face of Mr. Walrus.

"Here, drink it!" Mr. Walrus pushed a plastic cup into Cammie's hand. She took a quick gulp of hot chocolate and felt stronger right away.

"Thank you!" Cammie said as she handed the cup back to Mr. Walrus. She got up and looked around.

The ice, perfect and smooth, glittered around her, but there was no sign of the witch. "She's gone!"

Mr. Walrus nodded. "For now."

"What do you mean 'for now'?"

"No skater is ever danger free. All three witches you saw today hate skaters and want to destroy them. From time to time, they come back and attack. Fear is very common among skaters. The Witch of Fear keeps them from trying new moves and causes them to make mistakes in competitions."

"But we entered the password correctly!" Alex said. He stood to the left of Mr. Walrus.

"I know you did," Mr. Walrus said. "And the witch left both of you alone. But it doesn't mean she'll never come back."

"So we did our waltz eights for nothing?" Cammie asked sadly.

Mr. Walrus patted her on the shoulder. "Of course not! Having good, secure edges gives a skater a lot of confidence. And the more confidence you have, the more difficult it will be for any of the witches to attack you. Let me tell you something. The two of you have become much better skaters today. And very soon you will see the difference."

"Really?" Cammie stared at Mr. Walrus.

"Of course." Mr. Walrus took Cammie by the

hand and led her and Alex to his Zamboni parked at the end of the rink. "Come on. It's time for you to get to the competition."

COMPETITION

M r. Walrus took Cammie and Alex to the east side of the Sport Center. It was getting dark already, and the glass building looked like a large sparkling aquarium perched on a snow hill. A big sign on the door read: *For Unregistered Skaters: Please Register at the Front Desk.*

A cheerful receptionist wrote down Cammie's and Alex's names and the name of their rink.

"Why haven't you come with your group? The kids from your rink are already here."

Cammie's cheeks turned slightly warm. Before she could think of a good excuse, Alex blurted out, "We were a little late, so—"

"Come on, kids, I know exactly what happened.

Your coach probably thought you weren't ready, right?" The receptionist grinned.

Cammie shifted her feet. "We worked hard to get here!" *Come on*, she thought. *We have walked all around Skateland, been attacked by witches, practiced edges, three turns, and waltz eights for hours!*

"Okay, okay!" the receptionist sang as she handed them the competition schedule and their name tags. "Put these on your chest and go change. Good luck!"

She dismissed Cammie and Alex with a radiant smile. They exchanged happy glances. So they hadn't come to Skateland and endured all the hardships in vain after all. They belonged here, and they were going to compete.

Cammie looked at her schedule. Alex was going to skate before her in a boys' event.

"See you!" Alex said when they approached the boys' locker room.

"I'll change and come back to watch you," Cammie said.

Alex winked at her and went to the locker room. Cammie hurried to hers. She pushed the heavy door open and walked in.

Girls from Cammie's rink were putting on their skates, tying their ribbons, and stretching next to other girls whom Cammie didn't know. When she appeared in the locker room, every girl from her rink stopped what she had been doing and stared at her.

"Cammie, is that you? What're you doing here?" Sue Whitmore said.

Cammie sank into a seat beside her. "What do you think am I doing?"

"But Coach Louise didn't allow you to compete. Your edges are horrible!"

"That's what you think," Cammie said coldly as she retied her laces.

"Cammie! Are you really competing?"

Cammie turned around and stared into Margie Hilton's excited face. Margie's short skirt barely covered her fat thighs, but Cammie didn't care anymore.

"Good luck there, Margie!" Cammie said softly.

Margie's fat cheeks turned pink. "Oh, I'm so nervous! I don't know if I'll even be able to remember my program."

"You will!" Cammie said encouragingly. "You'll do fine. Don't let fear get to you, okay? Listen to the music."

Margie's mouth opened wide, and she stared at

Cammie unblinkingly. Cammie knew why. She had never said more than two words to Margie in her whole life, and what she had said was nothing but criticism. Now Margie probably couldn't believe that Cammie Wester herself was talking to her.

"Come on, Margie. Let's see Alex skate."

Margie looked at Cammie with admiration. "Alex Bernard? Is he your friend?"

Cammie nodded.

"He's a terrific skater!" Margie said excitedly.

They walked out of the locker room and went up into the stands. Cammie looked down at the arena and gave a squeal of delight. The ice was silver and smooth, and reflections of dozens of lights chased each other and formed intricate patterns on the glittery surface. Almost all the seats were taken, except for several seats in the front row reserved for participant skaters. Cammie and Margie found two seats together.

The boys' warm-up was announced. Cammie watched Alex, strong and trim in his navy blue outfit doing loop-loop combinations effortlessly. *He's going to do well*, she thought.

One after another, the boys skated their programs. Their jumps were high, and their spins were strong. Cammie began to worry a little. Would Alex be up to the high standard? And were Alex's parents in the stands? Had his father come?

Cammie looked back, then around and squinted, trying to spot Alex's mom and dad in the sea of faces. No, it was of no use; there were too many people at the rink. Besides, Cammie had never even met Alex's father. It was his mother who brought him to the rink. Most likely, his father wasn't really interested in his son's progress. It was sad!

Cammie thought of her own father. He always supported her skating and was proud of her achievements. She was sure Dad was in the building, sitting somewhere next to Cammie's mother. But no matter how hard she tried, she couldn't see her parents either.

"Let us welcome Alex Bernard!" the announcer's voice boomed across the ceiling.

Cammie clasped her hands on her knees as Alex skated to the middle of the rink. He looked poised and confident. Alex's music poured out from the speakers, and he began to skate strongly and beautifully.

Alex landed his first axel jump, then a double salchow and a double toe loop. Practicing edges must have helped because Cammie had never seen

Alex skate so effortlessly. He seemed to be floating over the ice.

Cammie clapped as hard as she could as she watched her friend take his bows.

The boys' event was over. Cammie took a long breath, trying to concentrate. In fifteen minutes, they would announce her group's warm-up.

"We're next!" Margie whispered into Cammie's ear. Her blue eyes were wide with fear. "Are you afraid?"

Cammie shook her head and laughed.

"What're you laughing about?"

"It's just. . . nothing." How could Cammie explain to Margie that there was absolutely nothing to be afraid of? Not after what she had been through today. Cammie had to fly across a ravine in a waltz jump, land a salchow on a declining road, and defeat three witches! After that, skating her program in front of a crowd of people wouldn't be scary at all.

Cammie's group's warm-up was announced. She stepped on the ice with more girls on her sides. Wow, she hardly even needed a warm-up. In the past, Cammie had always felt stiff and tentative at the beginning of a warm-up. Now she was relaxed and happy. She glided around the rink, wind whistling in her ears.

"Good luck!" a voice came from the stands.

Cammie turned around and saw Alex waving at her from the front row. She waved back.

At the end of the warm-up, Cammie waited at the side of the rink for other girls to skate. She was the last in her group to do her program. As she watched other skaters, she could hardly control the desire to get on the ice, to hear her music, to jump and to spin. There was no fear, just excitement.

"Cammie Wester!" the voice boomed.

Cammie spread her arms and rushed forward. Her music began, and time seemed to have stopped for Cammie. She was no longer aware of where she was. She no longer felt like a girl. She flew across the rink like a big pink bird with strong wings. Cammie's blades cut deep into the ice, making deep and secure edges. They flew off the smooth surface in solid jumps and swirled around the silver ice in perfectly centered spins.

Cammie wished the music would never stop. All she wanted was to keep skating. She couldn't step off the ice now. She knew that she belonged on the ice, and she felt like the happiest girl in the world. Unfortunately, the music came to an end, and Cammie took her final position.

The moment Cammie finished her routine the

audience erupted in loud applause. Cammie curtsied and looked across the rink at the smiling faces.
She saw Alex in the front row jumping and giving
her thumbs-up. Her mom and dad sat several rows
higher and were smiling and cheering. Mr. Walrus's
moustache twittered as he grinned at Cammie from
the back row holding the hand of the red-haired girl
from the Witch of Fear's rink. Next to him, Jeff, the
boy from Winja's rink, sat nursing his injured hand.
And standing at the side of the rink was. . . oh no. .
. Coach Louise!

Cammie's heart leaped in her chest. What was
Coach Louise going to say? Oh, she would probably
be so mad at Cammie for disobeying her!

Cammie sighed and skated to the board, slowly, uncertainly. She walked off the ice and grabbed
her skate guards still looking down, unable to look
Coach Louise in the eyes.

"Good job!"

Cammie looked up, shocked. Coach Louise was
actually smiling. "Good edges. You must have stayed
at the rink and practiced them all that time."

"Yes. . . hmm. . . something like that." Cammie
couldn't believe what she had just heard. Was that
it? Coach Louise wasn't going to rebuke her for dis-

obeying her? Instead, she complimented her on her edges. It was unbelievable!

"Cammie! Cammie!"

Cammie turned around. Alex was running toward her. "I won! Cammie, I came in first!"

"This is great!" Cammie hugged him. "Congratulations!"

"Yes, and you know, my dad came! He's here. He saw me skate, and he loved it! You know," Alex lowered his voice and looked around, "I hope he'll agree to pay for my skating now that he saw that I'm. . . ugh. . . not that bad."

"Of course he will."

"Cammie, let's go, the results are up!"

Cammie broke into run following an excited Margie. The official results of her competition hung on the bulletin board in the lobby. Cammie rose on her toes and scanned the page. Yes, there it was, her name, in the first position: *Cammie Wester.* It was unbelievable! She had won the competition!

Cammie screamed and jumped with joy. She had done it! Yes, her dream had come true. She was going to get the gold medal.

Everything else was a blur. During the awards ceremony Cammie really believed that she had come in first. The shiny gold medal hung on her neck, and everybody wanted to touch it. Alex yelled and danced around Cammie, showing his own medal to the people. Cammie's mom and dad almost squealed with excitement, congratulating her and Coach Louise on a job well done. Margie swirled around and announced to everybody that Cammie was the best skater at their rink.

"Well, now it's time to celebrate!" Dad said excitedly. "What an occasion! Our little Cammie is a figure skating champion."

"Yes!" Cammie clapped her hands.

"Okay, honey, now get changed and the three of us will go out," Mom said.

"I'll be out in a minute." Cammie ran to the locker room and got out of her skates. It was so pleasant to wear street shoes again. Only now did she realize how tired her feet were. Cammie changed into her jeans and sweatshirt. Her beautiful skating dress was now in her skate bag until another competition. Cammie yawned and hung the bag on her shoulder. She felt sleepy but happy.

Slowly, Cammie left the locker room and walked in the direction of the exit. The building was empty and quiet now; everybody must have gone to celebrate. The lights at the rink were dimmed. As Cammie passed by, she heard soft music playing from the speakers. She looked at the ice and stopped abruptly. There, gliding and spinning, was Mr. Walrus. As big a guy as he was, he moved as smoothly and gracefully as a ballet dancer. When the man completed a flawless three turn, Cammie saw on his face an expression of immense joy. Mr. Walrus really liked what he was doing. As many times as Cammie had seen him at her rink, he had never looked so happy. And yet the man wasn't skating in front of an audience. He wasn't trying to impress anybody. He was skating for pure joy, because he loved it more than anything else in the world.

Cammie remembered what Mr. Walrus had told her when she and Alex saw him at the main square with an older woman. *"I don't have to be recognized for my skating skills to enjoy what I do. Being on the ice makes me happy."* Cammie thought about those words and nodded. Yes, Mr. Walrus was right. It was not about medals. The true joy came from skating itself.

Cammie had a strong desire to be back on the ice again, gliding and spinning like Mr. Walrus. Unfortunately, she couldn't do it right now. Her parents were waiting for her, so she had to go. But tomorrow would be another day. She would come and skate, and she would be happy again.